STRAY VERSES

(SECOND SERIES)

BY

RICHARD SAUNDERS FENNINGS

*(President of the Piscatorial Society
of London).*

———

—

1903.

PRINTED BY
MESSRS. PITE AND THYNNE,
278A, KING'S ROAD,
CHELSEA.

To My Readers,—

Encouraged by the reception accorded to my "Stray Verses" published in 1901, I have ventured to present you with a second series. The contents of the present, like those of the preceding volume, have been written from dictation by my daughters, who have so loyally and cheerfully assisted me in my literary efforts.

The pastoral verses are the outcome of that strong inclination I have always evinced for rural scenes and rustic pursuits.

I have ever borne in mind the saying attributed to Dr. Johnson, that " he who neglected to pay a visit to the country during spring was guilty of an insult towards nature," and if I had omitted to listen to the sweet song of the nightingale and the cheery notes of the cuckoo, or to inhale the perfume of the may blossom on the hedgerows, I should have reproached myself for the remainder of the year.

The angling subjects may not, perhaps, interest some of my friends, yet they will, I hope, be acceptable reading to those who, like myself, are ardent disciples of Isaac Walton.

When referring to the follies of human nature, or endeavouring to raise a laugh at some of its foibles and singularities, I hope I have not offended the susceptibilities of anyone, but that the sentiments I have expressed will be received in the same spirit and good feeling with which they have been written.

R. S. FENNINGS.

34, Queen's Road,
    St. John's Wood, N.W.
Michaelmas, 1903.

(RECAP)

CONTENTS.

STRAY VERSES

(SECOND SERIES)

BY

R. S. FENNINGS.

———

THE OTTER HUNT.

—

The Torridge through North Devon flows,
   And scenery makes complete;
Once near that stream a place I chose
   As my holiday retreat.

The otter hounds, I heard were here,
   To hunt the stream to-morrow;
Their meeting place, the old King's Weir,
   Not far from Deacon's Hollow.

Was never at a hunt before,
   But thought it might be jolly—
So it was, and a great deal more
   Than dreamt of in my folly.

The scent at early morn they state
   Is best to track the quarry;
So up betimes, if I were late
   I should indeed be sorry.

That night J scarcely slept a wink,
   My feelings were excited;
I counted every hour, I think,
   Till hopes of sleep were blighted.

My window blind aside I drew
   Just as the light was dawning ;
Grass, shrubs and trees were drenched with dew—
   A perfect autumn morning.

A mist hung o'er the village green—
   Sure sign of pleasant weather—
Then groups of hunting men were seen
   Going across together.

I quickly dressed, with little care,
   And hurried to the meeting,
For many friends I knew were there
   Who gave me hearty greeting.

A pleasing sight first caught my eye,
   Upon a piece of lumber
The master sat, surrounded by
   Some forty dogs in number.

The " field " were such a motley crew
   As ever took to hunting ;
The parson, squire, and daughters, too,
   With village maids in bunting.

The welcome signal came at last—
   For which we long had waited ;
The master's horn sent forth a blast
   Which made all hearts elated.

O'er the weir, on a double plank,
   Our party then divided ;
Some preferred the right-hand bank,
   Others the left decided.

T'wixt hanging woods the river rolls,
   O'er beds of stone and gravel ;
You almost want stout jumping poles
   If on its course you'd travel.

Greasy and steep, oft on our knees,
   Along the bank we scramble,
O'er wrecks of ancient willow trees,
   Tall nettle, bush and bramble.

A mighty splash, then laughter loud,
   At some one who'd been tripping ;
It was a cook, so said the crowd,
   Who had a taste for dripping.

" Halloo ! " screamed out a rustic brat—
   We find he is mistaken ;
Some said he'd seen a water-rat,
   And ought to be well shaken.

At length we strike a likely " holt,"
   Dogs give the tenant warning ;
We were in hopes to see him bolt,
   But he was out that morning.

Now and again we crossed some fords,
   Or shallow bits of water,
And which we did, of course, towards
   Making our journey shorter.

A funny scene, absurd throughout,
   Was to our eye presented,
For men and women danced about
   Like folks who were demented.

They beat their heads and shook their hair,
   Then fled in each direction ;
A swarm of wasps, which caused the scare,
   Was dealing out correction.

Five miles, at least, we pushed along
   With little care or caution ;
I fear we were a noisy throng
   To make success our portion.

With hunger, tired, and almost lame—
   No breakfast had I eaten—
I, with the crowd, gave up the game,
   As we were fairly beaten.

Rid of our presence at its back,
   The merry shouts and laughter,
A " drag " was followed by the pack,
   Which made a " kill " soon after.

We to a roadside inn drew near
   And every room invaded ;
Some bread and cheese, with home-brewed beer,
   Was all that could be raided.

As much I did enjoy that meal
   As any horse in clover ;
Sorry, indeed, was I to feel
   My journey was not over.

For home by road I made a start,
   As warmer it was growing ;
The milestones seemed so far apart,
   And clouds of dust were blowing.

Arrived at home, fatigued and worn
   After my sporting gambles,
My hands were scratched, my clothes were torn
   In struggling with the brambles.

I'll play no more such foolish pranks,
   But round the country potter,
Or calmly fish the river banks—
   Let others hunt the otter.

A BUTTERFLY RIDE.

I'd like to be a wee fairy thing
To ride behind a butterfly's wing—
Jump in the saddle, and take my seat
With a bridle, bit, and reins complete ;
Cracking the whip, we gallop along
Away from the bustle, noise, and throng,
Over the gardens, into the mead,
Where I would dine on the clover-seed.
Now fluttering high, then settling low
To refresh my steed, and onward go ;
When we some jolly companions meet,
I find it hard to retain my seat ;
It's " chassez croisez," rein to the right,
To " set to, partners," you hold on tight,
A mid air dance in the blazing sun
Makes plenty of sport and lots of fun.
Ascending the hills, o'er mountain top,
Down in the valley we softly drop
To kiss the blue bells and make them ring
With joy at meeting their elfin king.
Back over the field our wings we spread,
Where the modest cowslip droops its head ;
Phœbus has fled, and the daylight fails—
To some sheltered bank we set our sails,
Where, under the hawthorn's leafy shade,
The lights are out and the beds are made,
And many a weary insect there
Now takes its rest in the cool night air.
As my palfrey to some vantage clings
I nestle between its folded wings,
To sleep and dream till the morning light
Has scattered the shadows formed by night ;
Then for my breakfast, some floral chips
With honey culled from the lily's lips,
Finished with sipings of nature's brew,
From buttercups filled with early dew.

THE KING'S POWER.

No battleship, cruiser, torpedo boat,
Or any of Royalty's ships afloat,
Nor the household troops, howe'er they may try,
Can protect the King from a common fly.

Should His Majesty feel inclined to doze,
'Twill settle, perchance, on his regal nose,
Or buzz in his ear, and cause him to blink—
Make the crown of his head a skating-rink.

These, simplest of facts, to the mind will bring
How weak is the power of my lord, the King !

THE TREASURE.

My wife had notice from the cook,
　Which caused her some displeasure ;
The usual steps at once she took,
Then told me, with a knowing look,
　She'd found " a perfect treasure."

Soon after this, arrived the " prize "—
　About her was no gammon ;
She caused my wife no small surprise
By asking if her food supplies
　Included pickled salmon !

At first we held her in some fear,
　And were a little troubled ;
I noticed, on approaching near,
She oft smelt very strong of beer—
　My brewer's bill was doubled.

My wife, suggesting something new—
　'Twas so much idle speaking—
" You can't teach me, marm, what to do!"
This, indeed, was very true;
　We found her past all teaching.

I brought a lobster home one day,
　To eat with bread and butter;
The " treasure " sent up word to say,
Would I to her point out the way
　I'd like it cooked for supper ?

Now, a hand of pork I much admire—
　A joint that's seldom beaten;
" Where's the peas-pudding ? " I enquire,
Cook replied " 'Tis on the fire,
　Will with the sweets be eaten."

She made seed-cakes, forgot the seed
　Curry, without the powder;
Each week committed some misdeed,
And seemed to take but little heed
　As we complained the louder.

We for sea breezes felt inclined,
　On making some enquiry
Cook said, that " she would stay behind,
To be alone she didn't mind,
　Might trust to her entirely."

A sudden call in town I made,
　On business somewhat pressing,
So to my house a visit paid,
Outside of which an organ played
　Dance music most distressing.

Inside I thought I heard a sound
  Of revelry and pleasure,
When to my great surprise I found,
Down in the kitchen waltzing round,
  A " Bobby " and the " treasure."

Now, that which most my feelings hurt
  Was not the gin and water,
But my best velvet coat he'd girt,
His partner wore the blouse and skirt
  Belonging to my daughter.

MORAL.

When choosing cooks, don't hurry show,
  Lest you repent at leisure ;
To praise their worth be somewhat slow,
In six months' time you perhaps will know
  The value of the treasure.

TO A SKYLARK.

Sing prettily, little bird,
  And in the sunshine flutter,
Let those dulcet notes be heard
  That thou art wont to utter.

Then Heavenward mount and fly,
  And extend thy graceful wings ;
Be a songster in the sky—
  The happiest bird that sings.

Carol, as thy soul inspires,
  Ere entrapped thou mayest be,
And against thy cage's wires
  Beat thy sides in agony.

" I. O. U."
(AN OLD STORY).

—

A farmer, having sold some straw,
Was forced to see his man of law,
For not a sixpence could he get
In payment of this little debt.
Quoth he, " This rascal will not pay—
Issue a writ, this very day ! "
On these instructions being known,
The debtor quickly changed his tone ;
Fixing of terms alone remained,
Which to the client were explained.
An I.O.U., and five pounds down,
Which made the puzzled farmer frown.
" Why this," said he, " will never do ;
It's ' He owe I,' not ' I owe you !' "

———

" WHIST."

—

Whist is called a studious game,
  Not a frivolous amusement;
It's principles have for their aim
  The reasoning mind's improvement.

Your expert's eyes are on his cards,
  With expression calm, unaltered ;
The silent game he ne'er retards,
  For his play is prompt, unfaltered.

If to excel you would aspire,
  Success would be your recompense,
Three things there are you will require—
  Time, patience, and experience.

Two golden rules you must observe—
　　First, your temper keep unruffled ;
Then strictest silence to preserve
　　When the cards are cut and shuffled.

For even if your skill be poor,
　　Be you ever systematic,
For nothing tries a partner more
　　Than the man who plays erratic.

There are some tiresome men, we know,
　　Who will argue, scold incessant,
And bully their poor partners so,
　　Till they make things quite unpleasant.

The grumbler, we all understand,
　　In his manner most depressing,
With groans and sighs betrays his hand
　　And receives your inward blessing.

Talkative folks are worse, no doubt—
　　Keep up a general clatter,
Till no one knows what cards are out,
　　Having listened to their chatter.

Another nuisance, you will find,
　　Is he who always hesitates ;
Can't for a time make up his mind—
　　A sort of thing which irritates.

Now one more class I've on my list—
　　Young giggling girls and flippant boys—
Who never ought to play at whist
　　But keep to childish games and toys.

———

THE CHARNEL HOUSE.

———

[In the year A.D. 456, a sanguinary battle is said to have taken place between the ancient Britons and Danes on the sea-shore, between Hythe and Folkestone, in which 30,000 men perished ; their bones, being bleached by exposure to the weather, were afterwards collected and placed in the crypt under the altar of Hythe Parish Church, were they can be seen to this day.]

———

Under the good old church of Hythe,
Death has been busy with his scythe,
And such a harvest garnered in,
Enough to make the devil grin.
His gruesome barn with bones is filled
Of men who were in battle killed ;
To view this sight I paid my fee,
And 'twas a ghastly sight to see.
Hundreds of skulls on shelves repose,
Placed thereon in numerous rows ;
The bones are stacked in neat array,
And in the centre packed away.
Sitting in contemplation deep,
I very quickly fell asleep ;
When I awoke, 'twas dead of night,
And all was dark, save one dull light.
I listened to the shuffling sound
Of many footsteps creeping round ;
The skulls had left their resting-place
And crowded round the central space,
Each to obtain a perfect set
Of bones which they could find or get.
Much noise and rattle then was heard,
Now and then misfits occurred ;
Many, equipped from head to feet,
Assisting those still incomplete.

The church door then flew open wide,
And down the aisle, with stealthy stride,
Forming procession, two by two,
They swarm each bench and fill each pew.
Solemn strains on the organ rolled,
And from the tower a death-knell tolled ;
Some oil lamps, dotted here and there,
Cast o'er the scene a weird-like air.
One then got up to try and preach,
But want of tongue, meant loss of speech ;
Now, that which much astonished me,
Deprived of eyes, they yet could see.
I thought myself secure, unseen,
Snugly hidden behind a screen,
When bony hands that screen withdrew,
And thus exposed my form to view.
Then quick uprose the ghostly crew,
Which every moment threatening grew,
Rattled their bones, clamped their jaws,
Waved aloft their skeleton claws ;
Half dead with fright, I raised a shout
Of " Mercy ! friends, pray let me out."
Stupified, in great alarm,
Somebody shook me by the arm ;
And when I came to lift my head,
To my surprise, I was in bed ;
My spouse's well-known voice was heard—
" Turn on your side, don't be absurd ;
You would have crab as supper fare,
And so you've had a bad night-mare ;
Judging from your sighs and groans,
You're troubled by the *dead men's bones."

*Dead men's bones : the popular name to certain parts of the crab,
said to be of a deletrious nature.

A WOMAN'S " NO."

Now have a care, be very slow
How you receive a woman's " No ; "
  You oft will find
  She'll prove unkind,
  Will change her mind,
Then her consent with smiles bestow.

I, at a ball, met charming Sue,
The rooms were hot, guests not a few ;
  Outside repair
  For breath of air,
  She did not dare—
Then afterwards relenting grew.

The night wore on, more people came,
And then we played some silly game ;
  Let's sit below
  Yon mistletoe—
  Now, don't say " No ; "
She did—but sat there all the same.

The end I scarcely did foresee,
I asked if we could married be ;
  She tossed her head,
  And firmly said
  She'd never wed—
Yet twelve months after wedded me !

" CATS."

A Cat's on the wall, which serves as her deck,
A meek-looking thing with ribbon on neck ;
She's now settled down for a morning doze ;
Been mousing all night, I'm led to suppose.
My dog has caught sight of her sleeping form,
And utters loud growls like a coming storm ;
He's growing irate, commences to bark,
He makes a high jump, but misses his mark ;
Then tries it again, " he's done it " this time—
A scratch on the nose results from his climb.
If one could translate the words of that tike,
I think you would say " you n'er heard the like."

ODE TO A HUMBLE BEE.

Be off ! you blustering bumble bee ;
I will not have you bully me.
Go ! take away that small bassoon
And play elsewhere the gay buffoon.
You cannot sting, howe'er you try,
Any more than a butterfly.
You store no honey—if you did
I'd know e're this where it was hid.
No doubt you do your lazy best
To feed the yonng ones in your nest.
But yet, may be, you have your use,
And do not merit my abuse ;
Then, in the sun buzz forth in song,
Enjoy your life whilst nature's strong.

THE SWINEHERD.

An autumn visit once I paid,
And at a pretty cottage stayed.
Each morn at breakfast, wet or dry,
A swineherd with his charge passed by;
And on his smiling pleasant face,
Contentment you could easy trace.
His clothes were shabby, worn and bare,
Much mended by a mother's care.
A small rush basket, light to feel,
Contained within his frugal meal ;
Some bread and cheese, or, for a treat,
At times a tiny scrap of meat,
An onion and a pint or more
Of watered milk completes his store.
Preceded by a hustling herd
Of healthy swine by hunger stirred,
Small pigs about ten weeks of age,
At what is called the " porker's stage."
Each day their presence is revealed
Foraging in the stubble field ;
And thither now they speed along,
Their language gruff, their perfume strong.
They reach their journey's end at length,
Where, putting forth his utmost strength,
The Swineherd opens wide the gates,
Lets in the field his porcine mates,
Who very soon begin to feed
Upon the aftergrowth of weed
Which springs up when the corn is cut
In every hollow space and rut.
'Bout mid-day they're seen to muster,
Side by side lie in a cluster,
Sleep, and enjoy the solar heat
From which their keeper beats retreat,

Takes refuge in some shady spot
Where he can watch the drowsy lot.
At welcome strike of village clock,
The lad collects his wandering flock ;
Out of the field as in a race
The cortége moves at rapid pace—
For nature's wants to them appeal,
Each eager for its evening meal.
Thus toileth he from day to day—
A cheerful soul on scanty pay.
Of those who labour for its need,
The world at large takes little heed ;
Looks to results, despising means,
To what is cleansed, not him who cleans.
To be as " happy as a king,"
No motto has a baser ring.
A monarch, with his hundred cares
Of public duties, state affairs,
Is he so happy, what think you,
As this poor lad with one or two ?
Some clothes to wear, and food to eat,
Health will his happiness complete.
His subjects, though at times perverse,
Do not intrigue, or, what is worse,
Conspire and plot against his life—
Make him dread the assassin's knife.
How oft have we in recent years
Witnessed a nation bathed in tears,
Lamenting o'er, with heartfelt grief,
The body of its murdered chief.

COUNTRY LIFE.

Genial Spring, we look for thee
To set the winter captives free,
And break away the chains of gloom
Which to endure has been their doom.
May ne'er thy songster heralds fail,
The cuckoo and the nightingale;
Thy floral gifts be ever met,
The cowslip and the violet;
In field and lane, on mossy bank
Primroses hold the foremost rank,
The first among the flowers that bring
Glad tidings of the coming spring.
Refreshing to the eyes are seen
The well trimmed hedge-rows clothed in green;
The leaves are busting into view
On shrubs, in divers shades and hue.
First to bloom is the almond tree,
Quite gay in its sterility,
Orchards present a cheerful sight,
Profusely dressed in pink and white;
From break of day, past setting sun,
Much barley sowing now is done;
With peas and beans, and clover seed,
And roots on which the cattle feed.
The poultry-yard is now alive
As swarms of new-born chicks arrive;
They hover round each coop and pen
Which holds within the mother hen.
The rooster, there is little doubt,
Is wondering what it's all about—
Greatly concerned is he to see
This increase of his family.
Weasel, stoat, and carrion crow

Watch the young pheasants as they grow,
And oft the keeper's gun is heard
When they attempt to steal a bird.
And now, well cleaned from dirt and grease,
The patient sheep yields up its fleece.
The spring-tide work is now complete,
And summer we prepare to greet.

We all regret to part with spring,
Though summer doth rich blessings bring;
Its cloudless skies and sunny hours,
Its fields of corn, its fruit and flowers;
The May bloom and the chaste wild rose
Which, with the elder flower that grows
On bush and hedge around the farm,
To rural scenes impart a charm.
The fields present a pleasant sight,
Where boys and girls take great delight;
Some go to work and some to play
At turning o'er the new-mown hay.
This is the time for shooting rooks—
A sport less easy than it looks;
Stoutly some country folk assert
That birds will all the trees desert
If yearly, young ones be not shot;
This may be true, or may be not.
All crops are looking at their best,
And hoes are now in much request
Amongst the mangolds and the swedes,
To clear them from the growth of weeds.
The grain is swelling in the ear
As harvest-time is drawing near;
Much beaten down are tares and peas,
While barley sways before the breeze;
Wheat and oats, which once were straight,

Begin to stoop beneath the weight.
Small rustic lads are shouting loud,
And ply their clappers at the cloud
Of feathered thieves among the wheat
Who come to pillage and to eat.
Reaping machines are working hard
To fill with stacks the empty yard,
Of which there will be soon a crowd
To make the farmer justly proud.
The gleaners search the stubble field
For ears of corn that it may yield,
While swarms of children round them roam,
Too young, as yet, to leave at home,
Where they would up to mischief get,
Or if alone would cry and fret.
There's still some harvest work to do
Which, Autumn, we now leave to you.

———————

The autumn tints are sad to see,
They call to mind mortality;
As human hair first turns to grey,
Then white, before it falls away,
So leaves change colour on the trees,
Ready to drop, 'twixt frost and breeze.
All harvest work is now at stop,
The turnip and the mangold crop
Has been secured and placed in clamp
To keep it from the cold and damp.
The plough is now at work once more,
Turning the weeds and stubble o'er;
Following close the ploughman's heels
The busy rooks find ample meals
From larvæ of the wire-worm pest,
Which farmer's lands so much infest.
Then truant boys and village sluts

Begin to scour the **woods for nuts,**
Whilst smaller rustics prowl around
Where blackberries are mostly found ;
Basket on arm, and crooked stick,
Thus they proceed the fruit to pick,
Returning with the spoil obtained,
Their fingers scratched and faces stained.
The squirrel now prepares the nest
Wherein it takes its winter's rest,
Having obtained, from wood and lane,
A store of acorns, nuts and grain ;
'Twere well if some folks laid to heart
The lesson which these acts impart ;
Look to the future, and provide
Against old age—man's wintertide.
The weather's growing cold and raw,
Huntsmen commence the woods to draw ;
So Mr. Fox must slip away,
To save his brush as best he may ;
The misty sun is circling low,
The air is charged with clouds of snow.
Grim Winter now appears in view,
And Autumn bids us all adieu.

Of all the seasons in the year
The Winter gets least welcome here,
For oft it brings within its train
Much human misery and pain,
Privation, want, and biting cold—
It nips the poor and kills the old.
Thick darkness, fogs and mist prevail
O'er wood and, plain, o'er hill and dale ;
The graziers now collect their stock,
And shepherds labour with their flock,
The lambing pens make snug and warm

Against the cold and wintry storm,
To tend the coming lambs prepare,
Requiring all their skill and care.
The frost has now possessed the land,
And all field work is at a stand ;
It makes the farmer look around
For other work that can be found—
Mending of thatch on barn or shed,
Hedging, ditching, pushing ahead ;
Lopping of trees, much work creates,
Making fences, repairing gates,
Bundles of small wood stack away,
And logs for fires on Christmas Day.
O'er frozen ponds the skaters glide,
While boys and girls enjoy the slide,
Or pelt each other with the snow,
Causing their ruddy cheeks to glow ;
The weather late, severe and raw,
Has milder grown, hence comes the thaw ;
The tillage once again proceeds,
And drills are busy with the seeds.
The season's drawing near its close—
Days lengthen, vegetation grows ;
A little sunshine—what a sight !
All nature seems revived and bright.
Long silent larks ascend on high,
Once more their tuneful lays to try ;
The song-thrush, and the blackbird, too,
In strains of love begin to woo,
While noisy rooks, of thievish tricks,
Steal from each others nest the sticks,
Quarrelling with the utmost zest
Before they settle down to rest.
The reign of Winter's closing fast,
Right glad are we when it is past.

EARLY MARRIAGES.

All nature's awake; 'tis Valentine's day!
The lark overhead is trilling its lay;
So warm is the sun, and mild the weather,
Deceiving alike both fur and feather.
The crafty fox, like the timid hare,
Thinks the time has come for courting the fair;
Rooks patch up the old or new homes construct,
Mid'st clamour and noise they steal and obstruct;
While house sparrows, viewed by farmers as pests,
With refuse and straw, build slovenly nests;
The starlings, who haunt the old chimney stack,
Lured by the weather, again have come back,
Where, year after year, they've brought up a brood,
Their peace undisturbed, good shelter and food.

. . . .

Ten days have elapsed; what a change we behold!
The snow's on the ground, 'tis bitterly cold;
The gutters beneath the eves of the barn
Are crowded with birds, much struck with alarm,
Jack Sparrow is there, his mate by his side—
Dejected and sad are bridegroom and bride,
Their nest is prepared, the eggs nearly laid,
All to no purpose, they're sorely afraid;
Their rashness they see, but now it's too late,
And all they can do is patiently wait.
Thus mortals repent—wish they had tarried,
Or waited awhile, before they got married.

"TENTING." *

Our Tenter may be 'tween twelve and thirteen,
Earns eightpence a day, small wages, I ween ;
Up early at morn to bring home the cows,
Who lazily crawl, oft stopping to browse.
Relieved of his charge, for breakfast departs,
Till milking is o'er, then once more he starts ;
The animals love the river-side bank,
For fresh is the grass—luxuriant, rank.
He watches them feed ; then, after awhile,
Sits himself down, the time to beguile,
Which heavily hangs, for the vacant mind
When left to itself no solace can find.
As a shipwrecked man, who's cast on a reef,
Will hail with delight some signs of relief,
Two or three comrades are seen to appear,
Soon by their presence the Tenter to cheer ;
Buoyant with spirits, which none can allay,
They struggle and roll like kittens at play ;
During the frolic, the cows he's forgot,
Finds, when he looks round, they've quitted the spot ;
The sun's scorching hot, the water is cool,
They've straggled across by the side of the pool
Where, shallow's the stream and easy to wade,
They're under some trees enjoying the shade.
The boy must look sharp, or fines have to pay,
For leaving the cattle to wander and stray ;
Then he and his friends are quick on the track—
After much shouting, the herd's driven back ;
As evening draws near it begins to collect,
Show's knowledge of time that's pretty correct ;

---

* This is a corruption of the word "attending," or taking charge
of cattle allowed by the Parish to graze on the road side, or
other vacant pieces of grass land.

Then making for home, **the boy** at their heels,
Once more on the road what pleasure he feels.
A stop at the farm, their milk made to yield,
The cows are enclosed and shut in a field;
While there they remain, no trouble impose,
The Tenter is free to seek his repose.

————

GRATITUDE.

—

Men ask of you, with cap in hand,
　Most humble is their attitude;
One thing they fail to understand—
　That virtue rare, called gratitude.

Having obtained what they desire
　Will go away, well satisfied;
No thoughts of you their souls inspire
　When once their wish is gratified.

Not heard of more, till once again
　They come begging with persistence,
And take offence, if you explain
　You're compelled to make resistance.

You, having naught to spare or lend,
　May prove a cause of enmity,
And he, you thought a trusty friend,
　Will oft become an enemy.

Be not cast down, nor weary grow,
　Such conduct brings its punishment;
Give what thou can'st, thy help bestow,
　And learn to bear discouragement.

THE LORD MAYOR'S SHOW.

The merriest sight for children, I know,
Is London's great fête, called " The Lord Mayor's Show;"
Let's portray the scene, imagine we're there
To see them enjoy the fun of the fair;
A room is secured, we'll say, in the Strand,
And luncheon prepared, with good things at hand.
The youngsters were up as daylight appeared,
For blocks in the street must always be feared;
Now see them arrived, excited and bright,
No sleep have they had the previous night;
Placed at the window, they sit in a row
Close watching the crowd assembled below.
With a surging mass the pavements are filled—
A mercy 'twill be if no one is killed;
Women and children in numbers abound,
While babies in arms are e'en to be found;
Pickpockets are there in search of their prey,
And many a watch will change hands to-day.
Medical students, in bands move about,
Who flourish their sticks, scream, whistle and shout;
Some fighting's begun, a capture's occurred—
" 'Barts,' to the rescue!" is everywhere heard;
These youths are but slim, and cannot stand long
Before constables tall, sturdy and strong.
"They're coming at last," we venture to say,
For mounted police are clearing the way;
The head of the Show's appearing in sight—
Gay banners and flags, emblazoned and bright;
Next, smart-looking lads, collected and cool—
Drum and fife band of the Duke of York's School;
Common Councillors, in their fur-trimmed coats,
Are beaming with smiles, enjoying their jokes;
With livery-men from each City Guild
The ranks of this great procession are filled—
Farriers', Skinners', Grocers' and Bakers,
Fishmongers', Cooks', and Spectacle makers.

Each Alderman sits in his carriage and pair,
A Beadle, his mace to carry and bear,
Belongs to some ward o'er which he presides,
With Deputies, too, and a Council besides,
Candlewick, Vintry, Lime Street, Aldersgate,
Portsoken, and others of ancient date;
The Knights-in-Armour, equipped for a fight,
Make the young folks scream and shout with delight.
Then, next on the scene, a life-boat appears,
Its crew receiving a volley of cheers;
Then *tableaux vivants* of the progress made
In science and art, of commerce and trade.
Enthusiastic now each one becomes
As band succeeds band with trumpets and drums;
The waving of flags, the ringing of bells,
While shouts from the crowd its excitement tells.
A gorgeous sight our eyes now behold—
In velvet and plush, resplendent with gold,
The coachman in front and footmen behind,
Two chariots of the costliest kind—
They are the Sheriffs, Joshua Hangem,
And his colleague, Alderman Slangem.
Hark! how they cheer, as they see him approach,
The Lord Mayor elect in his "ginger-bread" coach;
There sits by his side sword-bearer and mace,
His chaplain, as well, who has to say grace;
Quick follows behind the Mayor of last year,
A small troop of horse then brings up the rear;
Close at his heels, a disorderly mob
Confusion create to hustle and rob;
Much horse-play prevails, and heads become bare
As hats are snatched off and tossed in the air.
The sight's at an end, the children appeased,
Their elders, methinks, are equally pleased;
Things will fall flat, where'er you may go—
There's always great fun at the Lord Mayor's Show.

MINCE PIES.

Heavy suppers I hate,
  Avoid them I try,
Yet I find on my plate
  A tempting mince pie.

As my host will insist,
  Of course, I comply—
And it's hard to resist
  A dainty mince pie.

It proved excellent cheer,
  One scarce could deny;
Yet I eat with some fear
  The tasty mince pie.

.   .   .   .   .

What a night of unrest,
  I thought I should die—
'Twas a ton on my chest,
  That horrid mince pie.

POULTRY KEEPING.

Whilst showing a friend o'er my poultry-run,
Admiring the birds; when this had been done—
" They are said to pay, are they not ? " quoth he,
Though he looked so much like getting at me.
" I've often been told that they ought to pay—
J wish some kind friend would show me the way ;
I buy all the food, as you may expect,
Then purchase the eggs my daughters collect ;
To kill, pluck, or clean, no one is able,
When birds are pronounced fit for the table ;
So call in a man from the stables near,
Pay sixpence a neck and find him in beer ; "
My friend then remarked, with dubious smile,
" To make poultry pay, that's scarcely the style."

BUSINESS HELP.

If for assistance, you should try,
  And are puzzled where to go,
The golden rule is to apply
  To the busiest friend you know.

The man who has the least to do
  Will, with countenance sublime,
Express regret, not helping you,
  As he has'nt got the time.

This is the worst excuse, I think,
  By idleness suggested;
From making time no one will shrink
  Where he is interested.

KISSING.

" Why, my sweet, pretty miss,
    Look you angry and black ?
  If you liked not my kiss
    You may give it me back."

" Sir ! pray think it no crime
    If your kiss I retain ;
  I'll forgive you this time,
    But don't do it again."

  I am sorry to say
    Her words were in vain,
  For the very next day
    She had cause to complain.

  They're now Darby and Joan,
    And he's others to kiss,
  For two children they own
    Exact models of " Miss."

THE BOER WAR.

Thin streaks of light in the eastern sky
   Proclaim the early morn;
Around the camp the soldiers lie
   So wearied, tired, and worn.

With dreams of home, some calmly sleep,
   Others are restless found;
While to and fro the sentries keep
   Their watch on all around.

The bugle calls, rouse man and horse,
   Our scouts appear in sight,
To warn us that a Boer force
   Is moving t'wards our right.

Some outpost shots are plainly heard,
   And all's excitement when
The Staff in front send back the word
   To hurry up the men.

Warm work in store, these things forbode;
   Then comes the bugler's blast,
Warning the troops to clear the road
   And let the guns go past.

A flash! a crash! loud deafening sound—
   Their mortal course now run,
Lie men and horses stretched around
   A bad, disabled gun.

A farmhouse, nestling side the hill,
   Is burning fierce and strong;
Thick rolling clouds of smoke now fill
   The landscape all along.

The faithful watch-dog howled in vain
   To join the flying host ;
No friendly hand to loose his chain—
   He died at duty's post.

Making way for the grand assault,
   The guns to the flank repair ;
Limber up ! Right wheel ! Gallop ! Halt !
   Are cries which rend the air.

Our baffled foes no progress make—
   Are slowly falling back,
And in some dongas refuge take
   Awaiting our attack.

Creeping behind each rock and bush
   For cover as they go,
The troops their forward movement push
   Till close upon the foe.

Then, quitting cover, growing rash,
   They raise a hearty shout,
And, " at the double," madly dash—
   Thus put the Boers to rout.

THE DILATORY MAN.

He's ever behind
The rest of mankind,
   The last to rise of a morning ;
Has married a wife,
And dawdles through life—
   All efforts to rouse him, scorning.

Always " going to "
Do what's owing to,
   His work or duty neglected ;
At times he will seem
As if in a dream,
   Waiting for luck long expected.

He's never inclined
To make up his mind—
   The time for action protracting ;
Will walk to and fro,
Where idle words flow,
   While other people are acting.

He'll talking remain,
Forgetting his train—
   Many he's lost, to his sorrow ;
Will put off, delay
The work of to-day
   For that broken reed—to-morrow !

ADVICE.

Some one in whom you may confide,
  For counsel you'll unbend ;
But do not on a course decide
  Before you've heard your friend.

If true advice you would expect,
  Let him not know your mind,
Lest he your footsteps should direct
  To where you seem inclined.

When every one with you agrees,
  Mind how you go along,
As folk in their desire to please
  Will often lead you wrong.

THE CANARY.

Up and down, up and down, all the day long,
I hop on my perch to carol a song ;
My cage is of brass, and smart to the eye,
Still it's a prison, you cannot deny ;
The sparrows outside are sportive and gay,
I would I were there to join in their play ;
And yet it is said, I quickly would die
On being released, so helpless am I,
Brought up in a cage with nothing to do,
May be, what they say, is probably true ;
In future I'll try, contented to be
Surrounded by friends who make much of me.

"BEES."

Talk of our working man!—why he
Can't hold a candle to the bee;
By keeping still, you may contrive
To watch the inmates of a hive,
All working for the common good—
A strong, united brotherhood—
Free from trades societys' rules,
Fitly endured by slaves and fools.
Musing on my garden seat,
Well shaded from the noontide heat,
I hailed a bee, then homeward bound,
And asked him what success he'd found—
Whom he had met, and where he'd been,
If any novel sight he'd seen ?
Alighting down, he answered me,
" I'm very tired, as you may see;
On my wings from the early hours,
I've tasted o'er a hundred flowers;
From foxglove, lily, flower of bean
I have the finest pollen seen.
Many a mile I've been to-day,
Greeting old comrades on the way;
First I met was a bumble bee—
Oh ! what an alderman was he;
Fat stuffed within, fur clothed without,
He seemed so jolly, blythe and stout;
Humming aloud some tune he knew,
As he rose on high it louder grew,
Filling the air from morn to noon
With notes much like a small bassoon.
Then, shaking hands, away I flew—
Who do you think came into view ?

Blue-bottle Tom, seedy, alack !
Dressed in a suit of rusty black,
His coat besmeared with tiny shreds—
'Twixt you and me—like spiders' threads ;
He said he'd left a butcher's shop,
Dining off suet, steak and chop ;
Now was off to a grocer's store,
His goods to sample and explore ;
He looked so shabby, smelt so strong,
I couldn't stand him very long.
I scarce had time to take my leave
When someone plucked me by the sleeve ;
He wore a black striped yellow suit,
Slightly stained with the juice of fruit ;
Asked if I'd join him in some pranks—
This I declined, with many thanks ;
The wasp, he had a cruel eye,
Right glad was I to say ' good-bye.'
Now, strange, indeed, it seemed to me,
Not one of my companions—three—
Possessed a saving, frugal mind ;
But, eating all that they could find,
While I was laden, o'er and o'er,
With honey for our common store.
I've wasted so much time to-day,
So must be off ; excuse me, pray."
Then, bidding me a long adieu,
Entered the hive, and passed from view.

LUCK.

———

Frequently has my mind been struck
With those strange words, " Let's trust to luck ; "
Luck is a fickle, pleasant jade,
Whom careless, idle men upbraid—
Put not their shoulders to the wheel,
But ask a help with loud appeal ;
She is, forsooth, a broken reed
To count on in our time of need ;
Sometimes an unexpected guest,
With gifts to cheer the human breast.
Foolish the man who trusts to luck—
Sorrow by spoonfuls he will suck.

THE MONEY MARKET.

———

If there's a thing I do enjoy
    It is the morning paper,
Which every day some whistling boy
    Leaves on my door-step scraper.

Rather than miss this daily treat
    I'd go without my breakfast ;
The " leaders " my approval meet,
    My faith in them is steadfast.

About that wretched man, the Boer,
    I·read each scrap and particle,
And then I turn the paper o'er
    For the money article.

I find the foreign markets flat,
   And railway stocks redundant;
But more refreshing news is, that
   Money is most abundant;

And that it's being freely lent,
   The finest paper offered;
The discount rate is two per cent.,
   And less than that if proffered.

Between ourselves, I'm rather short,
   With my bank account o'erdrawn;
Of mining shares I've over bought,
   And a part of it's in pawn.

I found the bank was charging me
   At the rate of five per cent.;
The manager I went to see
   And to ask him what it meant.

He had a stern and solemn look,
   Yet a pleasant man was he;
Politely bowed, my hand he shook,
   As he then replied to me.

" Your interest I can't abate;
   'Tis certainly a pity
That you should pay so high a rate—
   You'd better try the City."

A friend of mine, who's " on the spot,"
   In my ear did kindly say:
" If you'd preserve what you have got,
   From the City keep away."

SEA BREEZES.

When autumnal solar rays through the courts and alleys
     stream,
Tripping to some seaside town is the city toilers' dream.

To ascend the winding cliff and rest on the chalk-bound turf,
Watch the shrimpers down below as they plough the foaming
     surf,

Or the seagull overhead, in its slow and measured flight;
Swooping down, it skims the wave and is quickly out of sight.

Thus it was I found myself in front of the mighty deep—
The heat was so oppressive as to banish thoughts of sleep.

Rising from my restless couch, opening the lattice wide,
Listening to the sounds that fall from the now advancing tide.

The hiss of seething water and the beaten billows roar,
The rattle of the shingle as it falls back from the shore.

Then cast the eye to seaward for that ever cheerful sight—
The flashes from the lightships which protect our coasts at
     night.

Mounting high, refreshing spray descends like the gentle rain,
While the balmy breath of ozone gives vigour to the brain.

GRUMBLING.

To grumble is the privilege
  Of we English folks, I ween,
And some there are who strong allege
  'Tis the safety valve of spleen.

We grumble at each pinch of shoe—
  Especially at the taxes—
Against the County Council, too,
  Our indignation waxes.

We grumble at the weather
  If too hot, too cold, or wet ;
That the season altogether
  Is the worst we ever met.

We grumble at the falls of snow
  If they whisk it not away,
And when the dust begins to blow,
  " Where's the water cart ? " we say.

We grumble if the trains be late,
  And we no allowance make
For causes which, I need not state,
  Will the best of lines o'ertake.

We grumble at the papers,
  And swear there's nothing in them
But advertisements of drapers
  For custom they may bring them.

We grumble at the gas account,
  Likewise the water-rate,
And as to coals, the large amount
  Passing through our kitchen grate.

Men grumble at their Christian name,
  Their trade, or occupation ;
I really think they'd do the same
  In any situation.

PERSISTENCE.

———

"A British tar is brave and tough,"
  Said Nelson to his henchman;
And if he fights on long enough,
  Will always beat a Frenchman.

Our foes have reason to deplore
  This stubborn, hard resistance;
For nothing can avail before
  Continued long persistence.

While foreign nations, ill at ease,
  With jealousy are raving,
Proud England still commands the sea
  O'er which her flags are waving.

———

FELINE GARDENING.

———

A cat is in my garden
  Transplanting mignonette;
No wonder if I harden,
  'Gainst this, my neighbour's pet.

My dog, of course, is absent,
  Or matters he'd arrange;
I can't await his advent,
  So now must try the range.

Then open wide the window,
  Pick up a piece of coal—
I've missed the mark, by jingo!
  And puss has got off whole.

———

A BLACKBIRD'S BREAKFAST.

A blackbird sat in a holly tree,
  O'er looking a well kept lawn ;
Was e'er a bird so happy as he
  Saluting the break of morn ?

Thus, for an hour, he warbles his song—
  Many a sleeper awoke ;
But ceased when the solar rays grew long,
  As they o'er the landscape broke.

Before he thought of his morning meal
  The songster enjoyed a rest,
Till hunger began to make him feel
  A vacancy at the chest.

"There's plenty of food," said he, "about,
  For some early worms I spy ;
I'll drop on the grass, and have them out
  In the twinkling of an eye."

He pulled out several by the tail—
  Who better below had stayed—
Then, "topping up" with a tender snail,
  A capital breakfast made.

THE NEW SCHOOL.

Men once to old traditions clung,
    Believed in King Solomon's school—
Bridle for the unruly tongue,
    A rod for the back of a fool.

"Proverbs," 'twould seem, suit not the age,
    Their soundness some try to confute;
They heed not the word of the sage,
    And the strings of his harp are mute.

To change human nature's a task
    Which many have tried to perform;
But are we the better, I ask,
    For their work of so-called reform?

The days of good manners are sealed;
    In our schools they seldom are taught;
For "cram" and "exam." hold the field,
    Absorbing the mind and the thought,

THE EARLY WORM.

"While you've lurked in bed, let me affirm,
    I've half-a-day's work done;
'Tis the early bird that gets the worm,
    Remember that, my son."

The son grew thoughtful, then looked wise,
    Replied with bitter scorn,
"Then how foolish of that worm to rise
    So early in the morn."

With triumphant smile, thus spake his dad:
    "Your statement is not right;
The worm in question really had
    Not been to bed that night."

THE CRICKET MATCH.

A tent is pitched beside the green,
Where crowds of idle folks are seen
  In a state of expectation ;
Our cricket club's engaged to play
The county team this very day,
  Is sufficient explanation.

The cheery sound of bugle blast,
A cry of " Here they come, at last ! "
  This, followed by a waggonette,
A dozen men to which belong,
Engaged in hearty laugh and song,
  While some one plays the flagolet.

A lot of brawny hands extend
With " How d'you do ?—right welcome, friend ;
  Let's drink to the day's enjoyment.
Now look alive, my merry lads,
Out with the bats, the stumps and pads—
  May success attend employment."

We won the toss, and then began
To send to bat our smartest man—
  But the first ball proved his ruin ;
It struck him on the finger joint,
Then bounded off, was caught at point—
  At this point our horns we drew in.

The county team were far too strong
To let us hold the wickets long—
  But misfortune has no limits ;
Two injured men had left our side,
The rest tried hard to stem the tide,
  Were discharged in forty minutes.

'Twas now our turn to take the field;
As " long-stop," then, I stood revealed
In the hottest of hot weather.
The balls all seemed to come my way,
" Drives " were the order of the day,
Which entailed much hunt of leather.

The welcome interval took place
And, though we are a sturdy race,
We want a deal of nourishing;
Huge joints of beef, both boiled and roast,
With foaming jugs of beer a host,
Was certainly encouraging.

Watching the play, much pleasure yields
To those who throng our cricket fields—
It was so on this occasion;
The players as they issued forth—
Some loth to leave the dinner cloth—
Received a great ovation.

In vain we change and change about,
Our foes have tired the bowling out,
And near drove us to distraction;
In course of time they careless grew,
While we our efforts did renew,
Till we sent them out of action.

Our turn to bat, we make a spurt,
But nothing could defeat avert,
Nor add to our list of winnings;
Although we made resistance stout,
Within an hour they had us out,
And thus beat us in an innings.

I went in 'twice, but made no run :
This seemed to cause a deal of fun,
  Which to me was most provoking.
To have ill-luck, is bad enough ;
No wonder if I cut up rough
  At this poor, unseemly joking.

The local press next day appears,
When of its vulgar gibes and jeers
  We are the great receptacles ;
It tries my feelings to degrade,
And says how well I've learnt the trade
  Or art of making *spectacles.

⌣ If on the published score, or list of runs, the figure " o " is in both
innings placed against the name of a cricketer, he is sarcas-
tically said to have made a pair of spectacles, which often
subjects him to much " chaff " on the part of his friends.

THE BLIND MAN'S DOG.

The blind man's dog appeals to me
As worthy of much sympathy ;
A prisoner, and a beggar, too,
Against his will, what can he do ?
Tugs at his chain the livelong day,
No chance has he to romp or play ;
Unable like his canine friends
To run about as fancy tends,
But, plodding through the crowded street,
Directs and guides his owner's feet.
Wears round his neck a small tin pot—
Which by kind folks is not forgot ;
And when a time for rest permits
By master's side he gravely sits,
Watching the traffic to and fro—
What are his thoughts ? I'd like to know.

THE FANCY BAZAAR.

Having to find a new abode,
  I made many a weary search ;
Till, in a pleasant sort of road,
  I found one near the district church.

I liked its service very much,
  And also the congregation ;
The wardens they behaved as such
  And deserved our approbation.

One thing there was that vexed me sore,
  Our members were not increasing ;
The neighbourhood was somewhat poor,
  And appeals for help unceasing.

We had a collection every day,
  And a most expensive pew-rate ;
The choir, of course, we had to pay,
  And funds to maintain a curate.

Church guilds and clubs, a varied band,
  Were conducted by the ladies—
Temperance, dorcas, mothers', and
  A nursing home for babies.

Rumours spread that amongst us all
  The church was falling to decay ;
We must rebuild the chancel-wall
  With but little or no delay.

The problem, as may be supposed,
  Was to find money for our need ;
A fancy bazaar was proposed,
  To this we at length agreed.

My wife was asked to help, and she
  To take a stall gave her consent ;
But afterwards, as you will see,
  She had some reason to repent.

To give my spouse her proper due—
　From labour never known to shirk ;
She wrote to every friend she knew
　To send her in some fancy work.

Parcels each hour arrived by post,
　Many contributions bringing ;
But that which seemed to strike me most
　Was the doorbells' ceaseless ringing.

Half opened bundles, paper bags,
　Are strewed on table, chair and floor,
While card-board boxes, packing rags,
　Obstruct the entrance to the door.

Cushions, fans and mats galore,
　Neckties, sachets—laced and frilled—
While things I'd never seen before
　My mind with speculation filled.

A van's departing from my door,
　The goods are gone, and none remain ;
I'm glad to be at rest once more,
　And find the house my own again.

See, the bazaar disclosed to view—
　Were present, " inter alia,"
Our vicar, curates, wardens, too,
　All dressed in full regalia.

The girls, by flattery or " flum,"
　And with mouths by no means mealy,
Not only got the men to come,
　But to spend their money freely.

They laughed and talked, they billed and cooed,
　Never dreaming of reverses ;
And all were in a happy mood,
　Till several lost their purses.

That through the dovecot's open door
　　Came birds of prey, need not be told ;
Of gilded sixpences, a score
　　Were found amongst the taken gold.

They on my wife were rather rough—
　　Upon her passed a stolen note,
Then someone took her sable muff,
　　Likewise the vicar's overcoat.

Despite these little tales of woe—
　　Unpleasant, as I must confess—
'Twas, while a very pretty show,
　　Financially a great success.

PET DOGS.

I'm very well known 'mongst the London " vets."
As the man who cures the over-fed pets,
Whose skins are filled with adipose matter—
Would certainly die should they grow fatter.
I've poodles and pugs, and dachshunds to feed,
With terriers, too, of every breed ;
They waddle about, as heavy as lead,
Before being brought to my little shed.
Tied up with a leash, for two days they fast,
Fresh water is then their only repast ;
A morsel of bread, by way of a treat,
And two days later a small piece of meat ;
In six weeks or so their fat is reduced—
Their owners scarce know them when they're produced.
When first they arrive, will oft turn away
From food that I'd eat, so dainty are they ;
But when they leave me, are glad to partake
Of things that I'd scorn to touch with a rake.

SPRINGTIME.

—

Arouse—arouse ! the winter's o'er,
  Let not your footsteps falter ;
Bird, beast and insect all adore
  At Nature's floral altar.

The blackthorn waits not for its leaves,
  But into bloom is rushing ;
The primrose bank its bosom heaves,
  The almond trees are blushing.

The feathered songster's notes increase
  In sweetness and in number,
The dormice and the squirrels cease
  Their winter sleep and slumber.

Spring flowers have now commenced to blow
  Their soft perfumes emitting,
While birds all brilliant to and fro
  In new costumes are flitting.

Each one is off to seek a mate,
  And, after much coquetting,
They make their choice, submit to fate,
  Great happiness begetting.

THE ADDRESS.

—

Parliament has its yearly treat,
His Majesty the King to meet;
From the Throne,
Speech made known,
Firm in tone,
Well chosen words, polite, discreet.

The faithful Commons hasten back
To talk it over, have a snack;
Take a turn,
Then adjourn,
Soon to learn
Who will commence the grand attack.

The Address to the Throne is moved,
And the occasion much improved;
Splendid voice,
Language choice,
All rejoice
The Speaker's efforts are approved.

The motion made, the fight begins,
The "Outs," of course, oppose the "Ins";
Cause delay,
Football play,
Kick away,
And many rub their moral shins.

It is further still contended
The Address must be amended;
Wild delight,
Irish night,
Full of fight
Till somebody gets suspended.

The Scotch must also have their fling,
Before the House some grievance bring;
 Members fly
 Subjects dry,
 Can't tell why
They were forgotten by the King.

The Welsh will doubtless have their night
To get their little wrongs put right;
 A free school,
 Like Home Rule,
 Pretty cool;
Thus Taffy keeps his wants in sight.

Teetotal faction, rather strong,
Want Local Option brought along;
 Do without
 Ale or stout,
 No more gout,
Or ills that to mankind belong.

Night after night the Members try
To thrash the subject till its dry;
 Air his fad,
 Every " Rad.,"
 Only glad
If he can catch the Speaker's eye.

At length the public, wearied grown,
Think much indulgence has been shown;
 Cannot wait,
 Getting late,
 Close debate;
The Opposition's thus o'erthrown.

Thus the annual farce is o'er,
Much waste of time that all deplore
 Drop the quirk,
 Get to work,
 Do not shirk
The busy time you have in store.

THE GREAT CITY.

If a curious sight you'd see,
Just come to London Bridge with me;
At early morn let's take our stand,
And watch the human stream expand.
Towards the City, pouring in,

Hundreds of thousands thus arrive
To swarm and fill the busy hive.
By eight o'clock, the growing tide
Begins to flow with rapid stride;
Warehouse man, packer, office boy—
The humblest in the great employ;
Like pioneers, they clear the way
To help the toilers of the day.
The hour of nine is drawing near,
Then thick and dense the crowds appear,
Composed of every kind of clerk,
The rank and file of city work;
Some hurry on, with anxious look,
Lest they miss the attendance book,
Which means a fine of half-a-crown
In offices of some renown.
Soon the crowd more wealth evinces,
Bankers, brokers, merchant princes;
Flowers their faultless coats adorn
From hot-house, shrubbery and lawn;
These are the captains of the host
Now hard at work, each at his post.
All striving with the same intent,
That is, on making money bent.
The City streets soon busy grow,
Messenger lads run to and fro;
Banker's clerks, with leather cases,
Speed along as if in races.

The brokers of the Stock Exchange,
Bargains with dealers to arrange,
Dart in and out of Capel Court
As if they felt that life was short.
The smell of soup, grilled chop and steak,
Feelings of appetite awake,
And indicate the time is nigh
When workers to their dinner fly.
Restaurant, chop house, luncheon bar,
The latter crowded more by far
With boys and youths in hungry mood—
All stand to eat and bolt their food,
They scarcely scan the bill of fare,
So little have they time to spare.
Then all is hurry, bustle, drive,
As more fresh customers arrive ;
Clatter of plates, of knives and forks,
Calls of " waiter," popping of corks,
Each pushing, striving to get served,
Manners can hardly be observed.
By half-past two the rush is o'er,
Diners resume their work once more.
As time approaches half-past five,
The streets again are much alive ;
Hundreds of men and boys appear,
To miss the post their only fear ;
Down Lombard Street they frantic tear,
With half-a-minute scarce to spare.
The letters mailed, so ends the day,
And thousands wend their homeward way,
By 'bus, or cab, on foot, by train
The wearied ones return again.
The sun is setting in the west,
Earth's greatest city is at rest.

COTTAGE FLOWERS.

I love the dear old cottage flowers,
  Which remind me of my childhood,
The scent produced by springtide showers
  On sweetbriar and the sutton-wood.

I watched the massive sunflowers grow,
  And hollyhock uplift its head,
While poppies made a brilliant show,
  And woodbine o'er the lattice spread.

Wallflowers, to me were ever dear,
  Bright harbingers of floral spring ;
Tidings that autumn's drawing near
  The lavender doth surely bring.

These simple flowers suit not the town,
  Nor gilded halls of vast expense,
Where hot-house plants adorn and crown
  The festive boards of opulence.

"FIRE!"

The sun went down, 'midst gloom and mist, left earth and air
      confused ;
A tiny shred of crescent moon its feeble light diffused.

The ghostly bat and screeching owl had left the castle towers,
Through shady lanes or o'er the fields to hawk the midnight
      hours.

The toilers slept their quiet rest, lost in pleasant slumber,
Awake by pain or restive brain ; sad, indeed, their number.

The old town clock in solemn tones proclaimed the hour of
    two;
A leaden sky the stars shut out and darkness denser grew.

A lurid glare shot in the air, a horseman galloped by:
" The farm's on fire—make haste to help! Now, volunteers,
    look spry!"

Some wind sprang up, which fanned the flames, while sparks
    in fiery shower
Whisked up aloft, or whirled around, all conscious of their
    power.

The fire bell rang to rouse the men, their number soon
    complete,
An engine, manned by gallant band, came thund'ring down
    the street.

But precious time had passed away, the fire had now caught
    hold;
To see ignite, stack after stack, 'twas grievous to behold.

They struggled hard to save the house, false hopes their spirits
    buoyed,
It's old thatched roof soon catching fire 'twas speedily
    destroyed.

Excited shouts of frantic men, as to and fro they flew,
The crackling sound and roar of flame more fierce and louder
    grew.

The cry went forth: "No water left!" the wells and ponds
    were dry;
What men could do was bravely done—no need to further try.

The sun which set the night before on such a peaceful scene
Now shone upon charred, smould'ring heaps where house and
    stack had been.

THE AUTHOR'S ADVICE.

———

When every ill is deemed a pest,
Folks of the worst make not the best,
While all around is much unrest—
    Then be thou calm.
When sickness, with its hundred cares,
Or money lost your purse impairs,
Make things go wrong in your affairs—
    Show no alarm.

When members let their zeal run mad,
And thrust on you each crazy fad,
Boycott the beer, which is too bad—
    Now have a care.
When doctors won't bid you adieu,
And lawyers stick as tight as glue,
False friends begin to flatter you—
    Look out, beware !

———

St. WINIFRED'S WELL
(Written in the Album of my niece WINIFRED).

———

In olden days, too long to tell,
The Pilgrims flocked to Holy well
To stop and kiss the wishing stone,
Whose healing gifts were widely known ;
And, at the shrine erected there,
Would tell their beads in silent prayer,
Or, kneel down in the water pure,
Some malady to stay or cure.
These customs, like the saint, are dead,
Not so the name of Winifred ;
May its possessor ever aim
To emulate its saintly fame.

A WINTER'S MORNING.

A wintry morning, bed's so nice,
  From it you're hard to cozen;
Your window panes are starred with ice,
  The water jug is frozen.

They've called you, but without success;
  At last you courage muster,
Jump out of bed, proceed to dress
  In hurry, scurry, fluster.

In shaving, one need scarce be told,
  To hasten means disaster;
With razor blunt, and water cold,
  'Twill end in sticking plaster.

You realise the truth of this
  Ere half the chin be finished;
Your looks, which once were not amiss,
  Are somewhat now diminished.

The toilet's done, no longer stay,
  Bedroom's quick forsaken,
While on the stairs you meet half way
  The grateful scent of bacon.

Before the glowing breakfast fire
  Your little dog's repeating,
With wag of tail, his warm desire
  To give you hearty greeting.

Then, through the casement take a peep,
  Weather wise inquisitor;
There on the snow, some inches deep,
  Stands a welcome visitor.

He wears a coat of russet brown,
  Waistcoat red—what vanity!
'Tis robin red-breast come to town
  Begging of your charity.

The fragrant steam from coffee pot,
   The pungent smell of bloater,
For such nice things he asks us not,
   Nor cares he one " iota."

He wants a luscious worm or two—
   We've none upon the table—
So something we must try and do
   To feed him, if we're able.

Some moistened crumbs of bread or toast
   Is all we have to offer ;
Of these poor Bobbie makes the most,
   And eats of what we proffer.

The scraping sound of garden spade
   Denotes employment given
To men and boys, who tend their aid,
   By poverty sore driven.

In time the snow is brushed aside,
   The steps made rough and gritty ;
Then off to take your daily ride
   To business in the City.

Though 'buses long have ceased to run,
   While cabs are scarcer growing,
To ride by train there's little fun,
   'Tis filled to overflowing.

The cold increases t'wards the night,
   The yellow fogs grow denser ;
To reach your cheerful home so bright
   Is quite a recompenser.

You hate the cold, yet dread the thaw,
   For what is more disgusting,
When cook screams out, with lengthened jaw,
   " The pipes are all ' a-busting ' " ?

COLDS.

Households have their trusty pill—
" Beecham," "Carter," what you will ;
Everyone you find can tell
What to take when you're unwell.
Should your chest with pain be wrung,
Have a care, and hold your tongue,
Or be blistered, dosed and pilled,
At the risk of being killed.
Colds, of course, you can't conceal,
Nor the misery you feel ;
All your friends will then advise
Remedies they dearly prize—
Eucalyptus, vaseline,
Camphor, nitre and quinine ;
Lozenges of every kind
In the chemist shop you'll find.
Doctors seem no more to know,
Than a hundred years ago,
How to cure a simple cold,
If the honest truth be told ;
Scarcely can such colds be cured—
As of old, must be endured ;
They take their time, run their course,
Patience is your sole resource.

FISHING.

Off to the river on his " bike,"
Whilst there he caught a little pike
And something else he didn't like—
    He caught a cold !
The fish he handed to the cook,
Told her to fix it on a hook,
The cat jumped up, and off it shook—
    Thus he was sold !

His eyes and nose were scalding hot,
Running like a watering pot ;
So that is all the good he got
    Going fishing !
He's still laid up, at home must stay,
He'll have a doctor's bill to pay ;
He would he'd not gone out that day—
    Useless wishing !

SPRATS.

Sprats come in on Lord Mayor's day,
So I've heard old people say ;
'Tis about that time of year
In the streets that they appear.
Cheap as food, these humble fish
Give the poor a welcome dish ;
Folks e'en of a higher class
Never let the season pass
Without eating once or twice
Sprats that they esteem as nice.
Some would of these fish partake,
But dislike the smell they make ;
" Gourmets " eat them on the spot,
From the gridiron piping hot.
Close with care the kitchen door,
Lest the scent should upward soar,
Thus the furtive meal betray
To friends who might a visit pay.

QUIETUDE.

You have some work you wish to do,
Requiring thought and study, too;
While all is still and silence reigns,
Is now the time to ply your brains.
Open the desk, dip pen in ink,
Then make a start, begin to think;
You've scarce commenced to write a word,
When all at once much noise is heard;
As by degrees the sounds increase,
You drop the pen, and writing cease.
From perfect peace, an hour before,
Behold a scene of wild uproar;
Small dog barking, caged birds singing,
Hall clock striking, house bell ringing,
Someone shouting, doors a-banging,
Music playing, pictures hanging.
You wait awhile; but, hope, there's none;
The morning's gone—with work undone.

SAGE AND ONIONS.

A frog jumped on an onion bed,
And to himself he softly said :
" How strong these ugly things do smell—
Who placed them here, I cannot tell ;
Their use to me does not appear,
They bode no good, I sadly fear."
A small white duckling standing by,
To his remark made this reply :
" The onions that around you see
Were planted for embalming me ;
When mixed with crumb of bread and sage
They help man's hunger to assuage."
" If that be so, why tarry here,
To live in constant dread and fear ? "
Then spake the duck, in boastful tone :
" For artfulness, let me alone ;
You'll always find me wide awake—
Not easy caught, make no mistake."
A fox in ambush lying near
Was heard to say : " I smell good cheer ;
There's little doubt that I'm in luck—
There's nought I like so much as duck ;
I do not want to have recourse
To sage and onions, apple sauce,
With appetite so sharp and keen,
My bones I crunch, or pick them clean."
Then, by the neck, the duck he took,
And out of it the life he shook ;
Seizing his prey, he hied away,
Wishing the frog a very " good day."
The latter soon did much reflect—
" This," quoth he, " I didn't expect ;
These onions, perhaps, were grown for me

When I am in a *fricassée*."
Don't boast of what you can't prevent—
A thousand kinds of accident ;
No one knows what his end will be,
How, where, and when, he cannot see.
Who would the future seek to find
Acts foolish for his peace of mind.

CONCERT MANAGEMENT.

In a suburban town I chanced to live,
It would be hardly wise the name to give ;
Suffice it to say, we can see St. Paul's
If the weather be fine and free from squalls.
The women who labour amongst our poor
Wished to show their zeal on a foreign shore,
To provide muslin skirts for the Esquimeaux,
And send overcoats to Borneo ;
In order to compass the " wherewithal "
Would a concert hold in the old town hall,
And they also agreed, with one consent,
That I was the man for its management.
What made me assent, I scarcely can tell—
They said I arranged these things so well ;
Now, flatter a man or tickle a pig,
And you have your bird on a well limed twig.
So I set to work, as I always do,
Showing energy possessed by few ;
They told me to keep the expenses down,
While they wanted a leading " star " from town.
I secured the " star " at one-half her fee,
And of minor planets, some two or three.
In arranging a programme, please observe,

You'll get more abuse than you deserve ;
For seeing his name on the top, too near,
The angry tenor refused to appear.
The French have a saying, well known, I ween,
That nothing's so sure as the unforseen.
'Twas to me an awkward slap in the face
When a small-pox scare broke out at the place ;
Two men, it was said, were rather "suspect,"
But in neither case were the facts correct—
The first being ill from dissipation,
And the second sick from vaccination ;
This report did harm, though checked in season,
For the nervous mind is deaf to reason.
Then, add to my worries this final blow,
The roads in the streets were covered with snow.
Next day, a messenger hurried to say
"Pianist ill, and unable to play ; "
The "star" arrived late, having missed her train—
These things were really a terrible strain.
The concert was good, as one might expect—
Even better, perhaps, in one respect ;
The audience, tho' small, I'm pleased to tell,
To give them their due, supported me well.
But now it is over, my mind is eased,
Never again to be worried or teased.
Like making a speech to a phantom crowd,
I said to myself, half speaking aloud,
"Put me away and proclaim me insane
If e'er I manage a concert again."

HOPE.

Hope makes a good breakfast—so it is said—
A very bad supper when going to bed;
The meaning of this would appear to be
We should not rely on futurity;
That hope is a plant of the morning light,
Which withers and fades at the gloom of night.
Proverbs like these are unable to damp
Or quench the flame of this radiant lamp
That burns on the altar of faith so clear,
The heart of man to encourage and cheer;
By its aid the traveller's road is smoothed,
With visions of home his feelings are soothed,
And in darken'd chamber, where lie the sick,
Comforting sparks will oft flash from its wick
To cheer the poor patient, restless and ill,
That thoughts of despair his mind may not fill;
Of hope to bereft 'tis sad, indeed—
No port of refuge in case of need.

" LONDON LIFE."

——

The season's growing into bloom,
For Levées and the Drawing Room ;
Court milliners, and tailors too,
Have quite as much as they can do.
Great care and labour they bestow
To dress each *debutante* and beau,
Young lords and men with sounding names,
Giggling girls and ancient dames ;
The latter on their persons wear
Ancestral jewels, costly, rare.
Oxford and Cambridge Boat Race Day
Amongst our sports still holds its sway.
Despite the cruel bitter wind,
This time of year you oft will find
Crowds for the river daily make
To watch the crews their practice take ;
And on the day fixed for the race
Thousands arrive, each takes his place
To see the crews go tearing by
Mid'st shouts and cheers of sympathy.
The boats are quickly out of sight,
And question is, Who's won the fight ?
When Easter's past, the Commons meet,
And every Member takes his seat,
The yearly budget to discuss
In lengthened speeches full of fuss.
Days are spent in ceaseless wrangle,
Till the subject's all a tangle :
Distorted facts, and figures too,
With mental dust obscure the view ;
And some forget, their passions hot,
If two and two be four or not.

Hyde Park presents a brilliant scene—
There, rank and fashion now are seen :
Carriages throng the ladies' mile
Filled with beauty and beauty's smile.
Where's the land of such resources—
Finer women, men, or horses ?

———————

The Cockney loves the Derby day,
Which falls about the end of May.
Sweepstakes he joins, bets pairs of gloves
With some young lady whom he loves :
If from business he can go,
He'll soon be off to see the " show."
Cricket absorbs the public mind,
And thousands flock of every kind,
Some to the Oval, some to Lords,
To view the skill the play affords.
The shouts that rise, the cheers that ring,
As batsmen to their wicket cling,
Under a hot and scorching sun
With heat in shade at ninety-one !
Which shows our taste is still the same
For this, old England's favourite game.
The upper ten, with pleasures bored,
Leave Town to get their nerves restored.
Thus we lose our aristocrats,
Now out of season—like the sprats.
The Session's drawing to a close,
The languid Members gape and dose—
And when " Black Rod " appears in sight,
They hail his presence with delight ;
A freedom from official rule
Which boys so much dislike at school.
The Courts are shut, and lawyers find
More worthy sport than human kind.

In one sense I think the nation
Should then bless the long vacation;
A kind of armistice at law,
Where hostile parties now withdraw;
This gives time for cool reflection,
Should their course require correction.
Excursion trains are running cheap,
Bring country folks to have a peep
At London, where the streets they walk
With open mouths, incessant talk:
While rascals oft their pockets pick,
Or cheat them by some scurvy trick.

———————

Now the season having ended,
Streets are up and pavements mended.
Owners of clubs advantage take,
Painting, cleaning, repairs to make.
The square presents a doleful sight,
Shutters and blinds keep out the light:
Caretakers are in charge awhile,
And with their children live in style.
This is called the silly season,
Not without some show of reason,
When editor's, for lack of news,
Thick pad their papers to amuse:
Or publish half a column full
Of tales well known as " cock and bull,"
And print one day, with some pretext,
What they will contradict the next,
Promenade concerts give delight
(For London's never empty quite)
To foreigners who frequent the stalls
Of theatres and the music halls.
Should the weather begin to frown,
The Cockneys hasten back to Town—

For men are apt the " blues " to get,
In seaside lodgings when its wet,
And gladly quit the dreary shore,
Home comforts to enjoy once more :
While men and boys in strange attire
Desert the warm and cosy fire,
And to some open space repair,
At football game to take their share ;
Many return all smiles and grins,
Others come back with broken shins.
With mud the streets are ankle deep,
And gangs of men prepare to sweep,
Clearing away the snow and slush,
The footpaths cleanse and gutters flush.
A yellow fog the traffic stops,
And gas is flaring in the shops.
The traders grumble as of old,
And frequently the Councils scold ;
Ready to fix the saddle tight
On any horse except the right.

'Busses and cabs do now o'erflow
With folks bound for the cattle show.
Fat, helpless pigs lie there in state,
Unconscious of their coming fate.
The sheep are pleasant to behold,
Well chosen from the shepherd's fold ;
With careful eye and measured tape
Their fleece is trimmed to suit the shape.
The beasts attract the public more,
Who poke and thrust and feel them o'er ;
The Hereford, rough haired and tall,
Looks well in its capacious stall :
While little Devons, smooth and sleek,
Are near perfection, so to speak.

The shops are looking smart and gay,
As tradesmen make a grand display
Of goods to catch the passers by—
For Christmas time is drawing nigh,
When labour's hours are much prolonged ;
The streets are full and pavements thronged.
Then country cousins come to town,
Arrayed in brightest hat and gown ;
And children count the days when they
With grandmama will come to stay.
But Christmas o'er, things settle down,
And quiet again is London Town.
Men with their skates the park explore,
Whose lakes are thinly frozen o'er.
The notice boards do not suffice
To keep the foolish off the ice.
Then reckless men and boys appear,
With just as little sense as fear ;
On they venture, one by one,
At first they walk and then they run—
Loud cracks are heard, the ice gives way,
And all's excitement and dismay.
But when they safely scramble out,
There rises up a merry shout ;
Then, drenching wet, they sneak along,
Glad to escape the jeering throng.

THE MISTAKEN LETTER.

My dear friend, Maud, with me is sitting,
I try to read while she is knitting,
But feel unwell, and shan't be better
Till I receive poor Charles' letter;
He informed me he would write to-day
About something that he had to say.
I'm sorry he's such a bashful man,
I always assist him when I can;
I felt sure last week he would propose—
He got half way through, then blew his nose,
Remarking, that he had caught a cold;
'Twas most provoking, I did feel " sold."
Ah! I see a boy come through our gate,
He's got a letter—now, what's my fate?
A knock—enters maid with letter-tray;
" No reply, Mary, you need not stay;
Dear Maud, do read me this letter, please,
I have such a trembling at the knees;
Open it quick!—what does it say?"
" It says—it says: ' Fish is cheap to-day!'"

DOGS.

A funny story once I heard
   About Turkey's greatest city;
I give the facts, as they occurred,
   In a " doggrel" sort of ditty.

Numerous dogs frequent each street,
   Unnoticed by the passengers;
Devour the bad and putrid meat—
   Thus act as public scavengers.

So rapid did these mongrels breed,
  'Twas resolved to make a clearance,
Conforming to the Moslem creed,
  Were it only for appearance.

Two vessels off the port arrived,
  And to the pier at once were moored;
Thousands of dogs the men contrived
  To catch and safely place on board.

The strangest freight that ship could show,
  Not worth to keep, much less to rob,
It crowds the decks, above, below—
  A struggling, noisy, heated mob.

A desert island was the gaol
  Where the canine throng were landed,
While three days' food—a parting dole—
  Was politely to them handed.

They died in sanctity, at least,
  Did these wretched curs exported;
Received a blessing from the priest,
  And to patience were exhorted.

The ships set sail and went away
  With all on board much gratified;
No drop of blood was spilt that day,
  So conscience was thus satisfied.

Much like the Quaker in the end,
  Who gave his lamb this comfort cold,
Said he: " I will not kill thee, friend,
  But to the butcher have thee sold."

HYTH|E.

———

Old-fashioned, stand-still town of Hythe,
I cannot call thee gay or blythe;
Cheerful enough thou art to me,
Who love thy scenery, thy sea;
The trippers most avoid thy shore,
If e'er they came, they come no more.
Naught to attract, how much they search,
Save in the bone-crypt at the Church;
Hundreds of skulls arranged in rows,
From battle fields, as some suppose.
Come organ grinders now and then,
Disturbing writers at their pen,
Or those who to their easy chair
For after-dinner naps repair;
The nigger, with his gibes and jokes,
Finds little favour with the folks
Who here expect repose to find,
And all excitement leave behind.
Upon the beach, young nursemaids sit
Watching the small fry as they knit,
While long-legged girls and boys abound,
Chasing each other round and round.
From houses close beside the beach—
Which lie within an easy reach—
Family parties cross the path,
Take with delight their morning bath.
For quiet enjoyment, peace and rest,
'Tis to my mind the very best;
A fine, bold sea and bracing air—
With it few towns can e'er compare.

BEAR AND FORBEAR.

To bear and forbear is the way
　To soften our passage through life,
To yield now and then, or you may
　Be ever in turmoil or strife.

My neighbour next door has a cat—
　A sorry poor gardener is it ;
Scratching up this, transplanting that,
　This creature I can't please a bit.

It has, I am told, vocal power,
　A statement which none will deny
Who, awake at the midnight hour,
　Oft hears its monotonous cry.

I possess a terrier tike,
　A noisy young rascal is he ;
For dustmen he has a dislike,
　With the sweep is at enmity.

His bark is distracting all day,
　But one thing I have to deplore,
He frightens our pet birds away
　And chases the cat of next door.

Such are the true facts of the case,
　My friends say I ought to protest ;
But just put yourself in my place—
　Pray, what can I do for the best ?

How can I complain of the cat,
　The course it deems fit to pursue ?
Methinks, for the matter of that,
　My dog is the worse of the two.

So neighbours must bear with my whelp,
　Whose barking to curb I will try ;
While puss in my garden may help,
　And nightly sing sad lullaby.

CHUB FISHING.

The angler, like his hunting friends,
Pursues the sport his taste commends;
Some for barbel, roach, jack or trout—
Nor must we leave the gudgeon out.
Should you for "chubbing" feel inclined,
To try our river have a mind,
Two hours before the sun goes down
You leave this pleasant little town:
Far up the lane, across the stile,
There you may sit and rest awhile—
Enjoy the fresh autumnal breeze
Which gently sways the poplar trees.
Then through the meadow lying low,
Where buttercups do freely grow,
And where the men work hard to-day
To snatch a second cut of hay.
A withey bed appears in sight,
Which skirts the river on the right:
Old willow trees, grown hollow, cleft,
Hang o'er the stream upon the left;
And all along, up to the gate,
Expectant chub lie oft in wait,
And thus obtain a goodly crop
Of insects that the leaves let drop.
Beyond the gate an open ditch
Shows you where to make your pitch;
In strictest silence stand far back,
Commence your tackle to unpack.
Long stiffish rod with upright rings,
Through which the line but rarely clings;
And if the current should run strong,
A slim cork float, six inches long,

Bright painted red, that you may see
To watch its course beneath each tree.
With well-waxed line, extremely thin,
To set to work you now begin.
A well-scoured " lob " proceed to place
On hook át end of fine gut trace ;
Then give a short but gentle cast—
The line you'll find will travel fast—
Control it well and hold it taut,
To keep the strike from falling short.
The float has worked twelve yards or so,
Now sharply disappears below.
Slight jerk of wrist, the trick is done ;
Your fish is hooked, now let him run.
He's in mid-stream ! pray coax him back
To where the water's calm and slack ;
And if he should the stream regain,
The line may break from over strain.
At first the chub fights strong and rough,
But soon gives in, cries " hold ! enough ! "
Then gently draw him near the shore,
He's in the net, and all is o'er.
You've half-a-dozen handsome fish,
And quite as much as man could wish.
Monster takes mean simple slaughter,
Which, of course, distress the water.
If you're in luck, a few retain ;
Put back the rest to fight again.

LIFE'S VOYAGE.

Life is a voyage all must make,
Though hard it is to undertake
By those whom fortune favours not—
The needy poor, almost forgot,
The cripple with his body bent,
The weakling and the impotent ;
These slender craft put out to sea,
Scarce knowing what their fate may be,
But at the slightest winds that blow,
They quickly fill and sink below.
Others as well built vessels start,
Complete in anchor, compass, chart,
The strongest ships that quit the land—
Like pigmies in a giant's hand—
Are helpless when the storms arise
And angry waves unite with skies ;
When Neptune's horses shake their manes,
Seize tight the bit, defy the reins,
Then out of hand, beyond control,
Snap in twain their chariot pole ;
Naught can stop their mad career,
They see no danger, know no fear.
Thus is many a gallant sail
O'ertaken by the cruel gale ;
Happy are they who, taking thought,
Seek refuge in a friendly port,
In safety to prolong their stay
Until the tempest's passed away.
Then, speeding on, they near the end,
The anchor drop, the sail unbend ;
Many are lost, too frail their boat,
Others contrive to keep afloat,
Reach youth, manhood, and some old age—
Man's last and final resting stage.

PATIENCE.

Patience is a gift to be desired,
But much cultivation is required
To learn self-control and how to bear
With fortitude each worrying care ;
But some there are who possess it not—
A restless, fretful, whining lot ;
Minds unrestrained, tempestuous, wild,
And petulant as a little child
Who some garden-seed to-day has sown
Is longing to see if it be grown,
Till, unable further to refrain,
Will to-morrow dig it up again.
How oft 'tis seen in trivial things,
And many a homely lesson brings—
The angler behind his roaching pole,
Or the cat beside the mouse's hole,
Each the supreme event awaiting,
With zeal and courage unabating :
And as all things come to those who wait,
The fish at length take the tempting bait ;
And e'en pussy makes her capture, too,
Of the plumpest mouse she ever knew.
When the harness chafes the horse's side,
We at once some soothing salve provide ;
So patience, a mental ointment rare,
Will ease and soften many a care,
When family troubles crowd our door,
And business friction tries us sore.
As years roll on, the shadows lengthen,
Our weakened frames no longer strengthen ;
May we ne'er give way to discontent,
But with patience bear the burden sent.

HOUSEKEEPING.

A housewife's mind is sore perplexed
  Providing for the breakfast,
And with her folks at times is vexed
  When to bacon they're not steadfast.

The husband, when the cloth is laid,
  Exclaims, " The same old rasher ! "
While glaring at the servant maid
  As if he'd like to thrash her.

" What is the use of sitting there
  Of fish and kidneys mumbling ?
Enough to make a woman swear
  Is this continued grumbling !

" One can't eat this, another that ;
  It gets beyond all reason
When I am asked for something that
  Has long been out of season.

" I'm sure I do the best I can
  To stop your being cheated,
And every sixpence closely scan—
  Yet this is how I'm treated ! "

Thus spake the wife, with tearful eye,
  Unto her lord and master ;
Who, softening down, made no reply,
  So the passing cloud rolled faster.

THE POSTMAN.

The class of men we all esteem,
Most useful public servants deem,
Who daily travel to and fro
'Midst summer's heat and winter's snow ;
Thus oft their weary footsteps drag
Beneath the postal service bag.
A mixture rare these bags contain,
Of good and evil, joy and pain ;
You breakfast, say, at eight o'clock,
And listen for the well-known knock.
You hear him first across the way,
Where he appears some time to stay ;
He's now next door, and then, "rat-tat,"
Your letters thick bestrew the mat.
Then comes the task of sorting out
Those for the master, wond'rous stout ;
New companies, trade circulars
Replete with full particulars ;
These in the basket soon are thrown,
Contents unread, unheard, unknown.
At one he glances with a frown,
It bears the post-mark of Cape Town ;
From nephew Frank, who writes to say,
To England he is on his way ;
So home once more this scapegrace boy,
His friends to worry and annoy.
For the wife arrives a letter,
Stating that her sister's better,
That Mary Ann, her eldest niece,
To be a spinster soon will cease.
"That means a nice expense for me,"
Low growls the master o'er his tea.
The daughter has some six or more,
Contents of which let's now explore :

Some things to vex, and some to please—
Luncheons, concerts, afternoon teas,
Claims for several small amounts,
Old drapers' bills, new dress accounts;
For " Miss " has grown well in her teens,
With pretty face, but scanty means,
Beginning just to feel her feet,
A girl of fashion, quite complete;
Affects a dress of lengthened train,
With eye-glass, fan, and châtelaine.
One thing she fails to understand,
Why servants are so close at hand,
And always seem so much perturbed
Whene'er the postman's knock is heard;
Much astounded to discover
Jane, the cook, has got a lover;
These matters give her great concern,
This lesson she has yet to learn.
Love is a power that's not confined
To any class, but all combined;
In silken boudoir's perfumed air,
Where sit the lovely and the fair,
'Twill often frequent, hover near
The kitchen's greasy atmosphere;
However strong, however stout,
No bolts or bars will keep it out.
Enough of love, which often brings
More trouble than important things
That in our letters are revealed,
But to the world oft times concealed.
Yet who would be without the Post—
The nation's lawful pride and boast ?
And ere the year shall pass away,
No one, I'm sure, will grudge to pay,
In mem'ry of his welcome knocks,
The postman's well earned Christmas box.

RIVER PICNICS.

Up-river picnics, to my mind,
    Are full of real enjoyment ;
You want the weather to be kind,
Some proper sort of friends to find
    Who'll not shirk light employment.

An upward route is my ideal—
    Affords the greatest pleasure ;
A row 'gainst stream you scarcely feel
Inclined to on a hearty meal,
    But rather take your leisure.

In such a trip I once took part,
    'Twas lovely summer weather ;
When full of spirits, light of heart,
We made an early morning start—
    A dozen friends together.

We had two boats well found in stores—
    A necessary shipment—
Some waterproofs to meet downpours,
Soft cushions, rugs and wraps in scores
    Completed our equipment.

The lads were all we could desire,
    Of rowing men, the smartest ;
The girls were dressed in light attire—
Might well a poet's pen inspire
    Or clever brush of artist.

We passed some anglers on the way
    In punts of long dimension ;
Sedate and patient men were they,
Intent upon their finny prey
    They paid us no attention.

The water's bright and somewhat low,
    Our steering skill much testing ;
The solar rays more powerful grow,
The scullers, who are all aglow,
    Require a little resting.

Near overhanging willow trees
    All gently cease from rowing,
And there awhile we take our ease,
Enjoy the cool and pleasant breeze
    That's on the water blowing.

Off again, but the wind's begun
    To be somewhat provoking,
So find some towing must be done ;
This oft gives rise to lots of fun,
    Much merriment and joking.

Towards some shelving bank we go,
    Where the passengers are landed ;
The lasses all turn out to tow,
The lads remain behind to row,
    Till both the boats get stranded.

Then, pushing off without delay,
    Once more the sculls we feather ;
The girls are singing, light and gay,
When suddenly the rope gives way
    And all fall down together.

First is heard a violent shout,
    Then screams and shrieks of laughter ;
'Tis found, when all are sorted out,
That no one's hurt, so set about
    To make a move soon after.

While pushing on, the line fell slack,
    Some cows were on the tow-path ;
The frightened girls all left the track,
And to the boats came running back,
    Fit study for a Hogarth.

With all on board, we forge ahead
    And find a charming station,
With grass like velvet to the tread,
And there our luncheon cloths we spread
    Free from all observation.

We almost had another scare,
    And were nearly put to rout,
As all were told to have a care,
That wasps were buzzing in the air,
    And some nests were near about.

The boat secured, all now proceed
    To help unship the cargo ;
From dock and Custom's charges freed,
Our hungry friends will soon succeed
    On it to lay embargo.

Snug in the open baskets lie
    Dainties in variety :
Cold chicken, ham, and rabbit pie,
And lobsters that refresh the eye—
    Food for good society.

Then drink to suit each kind of guest—
    Some prefer champagne to quaff ;
Many believe that beer is best,
Still lemonade is in request—
    Some delight in " shandygaff."

All hands are busy at the rear,
    And hampers soon are emptied;
The lads like waiters now appear,
And, with the dishes drawing near,
    Our appetites are tempted.

Some make a fuss, but little do,
    Like drones among the workers;
But that, of course, is nothing new,
For everywhere there is a few
    Incurable old shirkers.

The luncheon on the ground is laid—
    'Twill have a short existence;
The onslaught on it that is made,
By those who thus its cloth invade,
    Permits of no resistance.

The meal is o'er, things cleared away
    By all in combination;
Some through the pleasant meadows stray,
Others elect some games to play,
    Each to his inclination.

The kettle sings beneath a tree,
    An early cup betoking;
While girls with one consent agree
To hover round a pot of tea
    The men indulge in smoking.

We find and hunt a water rat,
    Which causes great diversion;
Much chaff ensues on hearing that
Some one wished he'd brought his cat—
    A very fine young Persian.

'Tis time we think of " homeward bound,"
    Make ready for departing,
Remove all *débris* from the ground,
That ne'er a trace of us be found,
    And then embark for starting.

Dark shadows now have fled the stream,
    The daylight's fast declining ;
'Twould by the stillness almost seem
The sun had shot his farewell beam
    And Nature left repining.

Returning slowly on our way
    We nearly were benighted ;
This pleasant trip, I need not say,
Each to his home did send that day
    Exceedingly delighted.

THE ANGLER'S PROGRESS.

Let poets and wits enjoy their joke,
And good-humoured fun at angling poke,
The capture of fish has always been
Pursued as a craft with ardour keen;
Nothing will cure the ruling passion,
Whate'er new sport comes into fashion.
'Twill engross the child at early date,
Increase as he grows to man's estate;
On his way to school at summertide,
Too oft he stops at the water's side,
Unheeding the time, to watch and stare
At the float of someone fishing there;
Then, hurrying on, he meets his fate,
By an extra task for coming late.
With much patience spent upon its track
He secures one day a stickleback;
So proud, indeed, is he to show it,
And let his little schoolmates know it.
His thoughts instilled with the fishing craze
Assume each year a different phase,
For the minnows, he no more desires,
But to catching gudgeon now aspires;
His ambitious views increase a-pace,
He longs to take the silvery dace.
The climax comes, for his Uncle Tod
Presents our friend with a fishing rod,
A case with tackle and hooks replete,
So now he's an angler, all complete.

Released from business cares and worry,
People to foreign parts will hurry;
But the angler seeks his native stream,

Away from the railway whistle's scream,
Thus leaving behind the city's hum,
A terrier dog his only "chum."
An artful little fellow is he,
With a look of sweet simplicity,
At his door misdeeds and crimes are laid,
For which his master has dearly paid;
The dog, as is his frequent habit,
Is off in search of rat and rabbit.
Through water meadows, across a plank,
You emerge upon the river's bank,
Our patient angler may there be found
With his rods and tackle spread around;
In the text-book of the angling art,
A great student he, and knows each part.
The roach are feeding like mad to-day,
And he soon displays a splendid tray;
Towards the rushes, around the ait,
He will sometimes throw his spinning bait,
And it oftentimes will come to pass
That the hungry pike are brought to grass.
With the May-fly "up," trout freely rise,
And many a speckled beauty dies.

An old man sits by his wintry fire
Watching the fitful flames rise higher,
Or becoming low and growing slack
As the wind roars down the chimney stack;
It is getting dark ere lights are lit,
When the thoughtful man delights to sit
And note the shadows descend or fall,
Flicker on ceiling or dance on wall;
By the fire asleep, his faithful dog
Reflects the glow of the burning log,
And stretched on the hearth enjoys the heat,

Resting his head on the slippered feet
Of his patron, whom he keeps in sight
Like a close attending satellite.
The master appears absorbed in thought—
Perchance he thinks of the fish he caught,
In the pleasant angling days now past,
Before he propelled his final " cast " ;
Ever and again you see his wrist
Give a short, sharp, peculiar twist,
As if in his hand a rod he took
And whipped once more his favourite brook.
The dog moans and twitches in its sleep—
Maybe that he dreams of chasing sheep.
This couple, then, in peaceful weather
Slide down the stream of life together.

ANGLING CLUBS.

Nearly two hundred fishing clubs
Meet weekly at the London " pubs." ;
One is known amongst the others
As " The Isaac Walton Brothers."
Its quarters are " The Angler's Rest,"
Of East-End houses far the best ;
Entering by a private door,
Which leads you to the upper floor,
There, a spacious room you'll see,
With tables placed for company ;
Around the walls on every side
Are hung, with ostentatious pride,
Glass cases full of monsters rare,
Caught by those who assemble there.
Great trophies of the finny tribe,
A few of which I'll now describe :
The centre case gains much applause,

A savage pike with open jaws,
Near five-and-thirty pounds it weighed,
But place of capture not betrayed.
A ten-pound carp, with vacant stare,
As if in wonder why he's there;
That bulky chub seems ill at ease,
He met his death by tasting cheese;
A splendid roach of two pound three,
Caught by Jones in the River Lea,
'Twas landed on a single hair,
Requiring patience, skill and care;
These cases, evil folk maintain,
Some fibs as well as fish contain.
It is a competition night,
When each one strives with all his might
To gain a prize, whate'er it be—
A sack of coals, a pound of tea,
At special times a silver cup,
And, once 'twas said, a toy bull pup.
First arrival, Tommy Seekwell,
In his craft has scarce an equal,
Is considered quite a marvel
In the art of taking barbel;
Next, an old and wary roacher,
Said by some to be a poacher,
Fishing wherever he alights,
Regardless of all private rights.
The members now all swarm around
An angler who for chub's renowned;
He has a large and weighty catch—
It seemed to me he'd win the match.
" You wait a bit," said one near me,
" Till Bob comes up from Slapton Lea.
I think I hear his voice below;
You wager he'll be in the show."
Ah! here he comes, and staggers in,
A little man with double chin;

He has a small, but heavy sack,
Said to contain a dozen jack.
Others arrive with empty creels,
Their want of luck the truth reveals ;
A tall, thin man brings up the rear
With barbel caught at Chertsey Weir.
Much fun ensues, and bets are laid,
Whilst the fish are being weighed,
If in the scale yon silver bream
At three pounds four will turn the beam,
Or who will carry off first prize,
Still full of doubt and much surmise.
On brisk discussion some are bent—
Form quite an angling Parliament ;
Others indulge in noisy laugh,
Expending all their wit and chaff
On some unlucky youth who failed
To land a fish he would have scaled.
The Chairman's hammer now is heard,
And silence is at once observed ;
The list of winners then appears,
And is, of course, received with cheers.
The usual healths are now proposed—
'Tis twelve o'clock, the meeting's closed.

THE SCOLDING POET.

(See a Poem called "The Islanders," by Rudyard Kipling.)

When folks take the world to task,
　Their statements should be accurate,
And its only fair to ask
　For language cool and temperate.

To the Colonies, our pride,
　We are accused of fawning;
Told, we cannot shoot or ride,
　And refuse to take a warning.

R. K., full of war's alarms,
　Says, in terms of strong dictation,
Every boy should study arms
　As part of his education.

He would dearly love to burn
　The football and the tennis bat;
All our public schoolrooms turn
　To drilling sheds—just think of that!

Cricketers he treats with sneers,
　Even " fools in flannel " dubs them;
Passing strange his wrath appears
　By the way in which he snubs them.

The Duke, being asked by one
　How Napoleon was beaten,
Said: " That Waterloo was won
　In the playing fields of Eton.

MORAL :—

Show a timid frame of mind,
　Your foes will try and master you;
Make yourself a sheep, you'll find
　The wolves will soon be after you.

THE DOGS' HOME.

Dogs homes in themselves are excellent things
To receive stray curs the policeman brings,
But to purchase one there, bear this in mind,
You've no guarantee of the slightest kind.
People compelled to get rid of their pets,
Unwilling to have them killed at the " vet.'s,"
Will somebody get to take them away,
And placed in the streets to wander or stray.
List to the faults of the animals named,
And cease not to wonder why they're not claimed;
Every canine vice is here to be found,
Let us step inside and have a look round.
The first is a collie, a fine looking beast,
Well worth the guinea they ask, at the least;
But for horse's heels, he's strongly inclined,
And several times has his owner been fined.
The next is one of the King Charles' breed,
Fit only to nurse, and dainty to feed;
The poor little thing is subject to fits,
May some day frighten you out of your wits.
This terrier has an innocent air,
Dirt cheap at a crown, and that you will swear;
The most spiteful brute that e'er wagged a tail—
A fact which its owner had to bewail.
What brings this pug to such a condition,
He's surely a dog of high position?
His habits unclean no one could endure,
Was turned in the streets as hopeless to cure.
Now, there is a dog you think you would like—
A powerful, wire-haired, terrier tike;
The most mischievous fiend that e'er was born,
Will tear in pieces your garden or lawn.
Now hear what occurred to a friend of mine—
A retriever bought for seven-and-nine:

This turned out to be the veriest thief
That ever did bring its owner to grief;
When loose in the streets the shops it would rob,
Costing its master full many a " bob ";
Jumped over the fence to the dog next door,
Ran off with his bones and wounding him sore,
Eat half a plum cake, an impudent theft,
And emptied a can that the milkman left.
It howled of a night, disturbing all rest,
Right glad was my friend when rid of the pest.
From what has been said, I think you will see
In choosing a dog, we careful should be;
Animals' habits first ascertain,
Rejecting the one that's too old to train.

THE MOUSE'S LAMENT.

I reside in a West-End house,
　　Where there's a well-filled larder kept,
And who's to blame a hungry mouse
　　If frequently inside he crept ?

Not a friend in the world have I,
　　Though small is the wrong that I do,
For my life I've often to fly
　　From the cat and the servants, too.

How trifles will cause an alarm,
　　Put the boldest of men to flight,
When there's not the slightest of harm
　　In the object causing the fright ?

I'm the most timid creature made,
　　Yet 'tis the strangest sight to see
How much the ladies are afraid
　　Of such a little one as me.

The other night I ventured forth
  Some victuals to find or steal,
Crumbs which fall from the supper cloth
  Are with me a favourite meal.

The family were sitting late,
  Enjoying their evening chat,
The fire had vanished from the grate,
  So had my foe, the household cat.

It happened that I was found out,
  Amidst shrieks of alarm and fright ;
" A mouse—a mouse !" each one did shout,
  As I disappeared from sight.

Each female mounted on a chair,
  All confusion, noise and scuffle,
The men amused, joined in the scare
  With the poker, tongs and shovel.

I narrowly escaped my doom,
  And had still further cause to dread,
The cat they locked up in the room,
  Which sent me supperless to bed.

My enemies no rest do give,
  I'm driven from pillar to post ;
It cannot be said that I live,
  I only exist at the most.

No office my life would insure,
  Its agents would laugh me to scorn ;
The troubles I have to endure
  Make me wish I'd never been born.

AUTUMN MORNING.

The moon has faded out of sight,
The morning star is shining bright,
While misty, frost-like dews prevail
Covering with moisture hill and dale ;
The roadside hedges, bare of leaf,
Show spider's webs in strong relief ;
A gloomy silence reigns around,
Unbroken by the slightest sound,
'Till fitful, twittering notes are heard
To issue from that early bird—
The robin—who has just awoke,
To chide and call the sleeping folk.
The dairy-maid gets up with speed,
The cows to milk, the pigs to feed ;
Unlock the poultry house, release
The noisy ducks and grumbling geese ;
Come men and boys with heavy tread,
The latter loth to leave their bed.
The stable doors are open wide,
And horses soon are brought outside ;
Then all proceed across the weald
To plough again the stubble field ;
A rustic guides the leading horse,
And thus ensures an even course.
The busy rooks, a-circling round,
Investigate the upturned ground,
On grub and beetle swiftly drop,
Which often saves the growing crop.
Both men and beast now weary feel,
And rest to take their morning meal ;
The sun is smiling on the scene,
For Autumn now is nature's queen.

THE BANK MANAGER.

If you be willing, I'll contrive
To show you o'er a banking hive :
At stroke of nine appears each clerk,
The manager begins his work,
Unlocks the safe, thus amply fills
With notes and coin the cashiers' tills ;
Opens his letters, takes a glance
To see how stocks or shares advance.
Next, deals with matters of finance
Without a tincture of romance ;
And on this rule he learns to act—
Six statements do not make one fact.
For " hard-ups " he has special care—
As to the banks such men repair—
Knows how to diagnose each case,
Its origin and progress trace.
Should they the bank's assistance seek
To stop a hole, or close a leak,
He'll shake his head, express regret
That their desires cannot be met,
As bankers only lend to those
With whom the tide of fortune flows.
Amongst the clients ever found,
Urbane, polite to all around ;
Some few are troublesome, no doubt,
For six months keep their pass-books out,
Then, bustle in one busy day,
To have it made up while they stay.
Others, a Saturday will choose,
When he has little time to lose,
To interview and pick his brain,
And with him for an hour remain.
But patient, calm, unruffled he—
A stoic in philosophy—
Listens to all they've got to say,

THE THAMES TROUT.

"The feast of fools," some folks may say,
Is a most appropriate day
For Thames trout fishing to commence ;
True enough, in a certain sense,
Though ever since the world began
The fish is fooled, not oft the man.
The trout in winter torpid lie
In deepest holes, all food deny
Until the spring, when, lean and gaunt,
They seek again their favourite haunt
Beneath some half-sunk roots of trees ;
There—lie in wait their prey to seize—
They quick recover, growing fat
On minnow and fresh water sprat ;
For should the weather set in warm
The bleak will then begin to swarm,
Heading up stream they soon appear
Darting about the boiling weir ;
And, as they in the foam disport,
May with a hand-net oft be caught.
The trout then follow up the bleak,
Where round the weir they lurk and sleep ;
A monster now is "on the feed,"
Across the pool, at lightning speed,
He dashes at a group of fry,
Who out of water madly fly,
Try to avoid their fate in vain,
Are caught as they fall back again.
This scene did not escape the eye
Of Angler Ford, who, standing by,
Had kept a long and sharp look out
To watch the feeding of the trout.
This crafty man next day proceeds
To spin the pool—now free of weeds ;

Notes well the spot where yesterday
He saw the trout pursue its prey ;
He makes a cast, gets no reply,
A second and a third doth try—
A rush ! a tug ! no time to wait,
He finds a fish has seized his bait ;
His winch goes round with rapid speed—
To check it would be bad, indeed ;
Some sixty yards have now been spent,
And the pliant rod's no longer bent,
To regain the line, not lose touch,
Often the Tyro puzzles much.
Quiet the fish must not remain,
Draw tight the line, then loose again
As up the stream he makes a dash
And leaps out with a mighty splash ;
To keep it from the sunken piles
Requires the angler's skill and wiles.
The fish's strength decreases fast,
The conflict now is o'er and past ;
A grand old fish has ceased to rule
As monarch of the seething pool.

FADS AND FANCIES.

In this world are many things
   Confusing, strange and vexing ;
Each year some new doctrine brings
   To human minds perplexing.

There's no limit, we are told,
   To novelties in science ;
New ideas usurp the old
   On which we placed reliance.

Fads and fancies still abound,
 No sign show of reduction;
Honest folks are ever found
 To give us kind instruction—

What to drink and what to eat,
 Physic in time of sickness,
Clothes to wear, in cold or heat,
 Their texture, shape or thickness.

One would stop our mutton chop,
 And draw the line e'en closer—
Shut up every butcher's shop
 And make him turn greengrocer.

He would regulate the " Zoo.,"
 Feed inmates on low diet,
Give them something mild to chew
 To keep them tame and quiet.

Swede turnips he would try on
 The python from the Niger;
And cauliflowers rely on
 To feed the hungry tiger.

Nuts for monkeys would remain,
 For cockatoos and parrots;
But the eagles might disdain
 A meal of garden carrots.

Listen to our liquid friend
 Unfold the water question,
With a zeal that knows no end;
 Now this is his suggestion :

" If your health you would preserve
 Sign the pledge or protocol;
This commandment to observe—
 Thou shalt drink no alcohol."

On food nourishment he's read,
  (The statement's somewhat risky),
More is in an ounce of bread
  Than in a quart of whisky.

Homeopathy, you'll find,
  Is by the ladies favoured;
Ills to cure of every kind,
  Have many worked and laboured.

See a chest filled to the top
  With bottles neatly labelled,
From this little chemist shop
  Dispense they when enabled.

If an ailment you disclose,
  Their kind sympathies you'll touch ;
Take whatever they propose—
  It will scarcely matter much.

It won't hurt you, yet the dame—
  Young, middle-aged or ancient—
Will your friendship ever claim,
  A convert and a patient.

The allopathist loud affirms
  His doctrine is conclusive ;
Herbalists, in trenchant terms,
  Denounce it as delusive.

New religious sects are met—
  Faith-healing, Christian Science—
All our former notions set
  Completely at defiance.

So we thus are borne along ;
  It is difficult to see
Who is right or who is wrong
  When our doctors disagree.

THE BUDGET.

When Eastertide is drawing near,
The Parliament expects to hear
The Ministers' yearly statement
Of the increase or abatement
Of duties, taxes, impost rates,
Army and Navy estimates;
Shrewd speculations now ensue
As to the course he will pursue,
While all the merchants are afraid
Of some disturbance in their trade,
They, panic-stricken, then despond,
And quickly clear their goods from bond.
'Tis now the gossip of the clubs,
Of coffee tavern, village " pubs.";
'Tis much discussed in railway train,
Where some endeavour to explain
Views to suit their own position,
Trade, profession or condition;
Expose the selfishness they feel,
Regardless of the common weal.
Beer drinkers and abstainers, too,
Create a noise, make much ado;
The former, in their wrath, would shut
The latter in his water-butt,
And he, in turn, would never shrink
From doubling every tax on drink;
The papers they have much to say
On fiscal problems of the day.
In time the Budget comes to light,
And then occurs a party fight;
Scoffing " Rads." and heated " Tories "
Tell again the well known stories:
One proclaims direct taxation
As best suited to the nation,

The other favours indirect—
Being, they say, the more correct.
The Members kick the Bill about,
Until the subject's well thrashed out ;
At length they let the measure pass—
Quiet again is every class,
From champions of beer or tea,
To victims under Schedule " D."

THE POLICE COURT.

At police courts, on a Monday morn,
Awaiting to be heard or sworn,
You'll see a group of people stand—
A seedy, shabby-looking band ;
In time the door is opened wide,
The court is quickly filled inside ;
The crowd to silence being brought,
The magistrate walks into court.
With manners calm and air discreet,
Upon the bench he takes his seat ;
Ably assisted by his clerk,
He very quickly gets to work.
Some transfer licenses to sign
For selling spirits, beer and wine,
And many affidavits, too,
Are in his presence sworn as true ;
When rid of these and minor things
The business proper then begins.
First to appear, on sad parade,
What is called the " Black-eyed Brigade,"
Who now complain, with sob and tear,
Of brutal husbands whom they fear,
And some a summons will obtain,
Who'll ne'er approach the court again ;

As in the higher grades of life,
Is woman's weakness ever rife.
Tiresome lodgers next are heard
On quarrels only too absurd ;
His Worship's patience oft they try
When for a summons they apply.
Night charges now possess the field,
And some amusement seem to yield ;
The jailer, like an M.C. taught,
Prepares his programme for the court ;
With countenance unmoved and stern
He brings each prisoner up in turn.
Crestfallen, and in sorry plight,
Appear these captures of the night ;
Here drunken men of every grade,
Pickpockets, busy at their trade,
Mix with young students on the spree
And roysterers who can't agree ;
But, sad to see, I must confess,
Are women in their wretchedness.
His worship's skill is here displayed,
And rapid progress soon is made ;
Justice dispensed on even lines,
Some to prison, but most to fines ;
Case after case is thus dispatched
With promptitude but rarely matched.
The *Black Maria then takes away
Unfortunates that cannot pay ;
This brings the day's work to a close—
A record strange of human woes.

     *Police Van.

FOLK-LORE.

Of fears that haunt poor human kind,
  Superstition is the strongest,
'Tis harboured by the timid mind,
  And with it remains the longest.

In olden time witchcraft was rife,
  Diviners of dreams respected,
Stories told of animal life—
  A few of which I've selected.

A dog sees death enter a house,
  That hedgehogs milk cows they declare,
The shrew's a bewitched evil mouse,
  And eels are produced from horse hair.

Should a grey crow their pathway cross,
  Let anglers no further proceed—
But if they meet a piebald horse,
  The catch will be heavy indeed.

When death occurs in a house, one sees
  Men draping the bee hives with crape,
Then on their knees inform the bees,
  Lest they should make good their escape.

If hares cross your path, they vow,
  'Twill bring disappointment bitter;
The same may be said of a sow,
  Unless she has with her a litter.

When a ship is about to sail,
  Puss makes but a bad impression,
She's a gale of wind in her tail
  Is the seaman's odd expression.

The raven, screech owl and the cat,
   When to dismal cries resorting,
Foul weather means—though some think that
   'Tis their noisy way of courting.

A cricket in the house brings luck;
   And of cash you'll be a winner
If in your purse a spider chuck,
   Well known as the money spinner.

Blood sucked from living moles will cure
   Epileptic fits distressing,
While the brain of a hare is sure
   To sick infants prove a blessing.

The writer now kind pardon begs
   If your credence should be shaken—
They say that where the cock lays eggs
   The hens lay rashers of bacon.

MATRIMONIAL WRECK.

Bob had led a bachelor's life,
Ne'er had thought of taking a wife;
As years rolled on, and time had flown,
He found himself almost alone.
Most of his oldest chums had wed,
Amongst them Harry, Tom, and Fred;
He now began to think it time
To make a change whilst in his prime.
Scarcely ready to embark yet,
Thought he would consult the market;

A spinster of uncertain age
His first attention did engage;
With pleasing manners, highly bred,
And lots of money—so 'twas said.
Bob, much concerned about her wealth,
Then learns this piece of news by stealth:
That all her cash in trust was held,
Which very soon his ardour quelled;
So, after all the court he'd paid,
He ran off with her waiting-maid.
But Nemesis o'ertook our friend,
Who was sore punished in the end.
A few short months had run their course
When Bob commenced to feel remorse;
As dim became the nuptial fire,
The wretched pair began to tire,
And love no more their brains befogs,
For now they fight like cats and dogs.
Things would ne'er have reached this high state
Had our man been sworn at Highgate;
This swearing is of ancient date,
The oath to take I here may state:
"To never kiss the waiting-maid
When you the mistress can invade;
To pour the small beer down the sink
If you can get strong ale to drink;
From brown bread always to abstain,
If good white loaves you can obtain."

LONDON COUNTY COUNCIL.

When county councils first were known,
London was getting overgrown;
   Reform immense,
   In every sense,
   At small expense,
'Twas said would very soon be shown.

Their task was to administrate:
But they would like to legislate,
   Thus undertake
   New laws to make,
   Strong measures take
Their ruling skill to illustrate.

The Council we at first possessed,
It did some good, must be confessed :
   The streets made clean,
   More lamps were seen
   Than yet had been,
And sanitation wrongs redressed.

But much has happened since that day,
And things have changed, I grieve to say;
   New men elect,
   Good work expect,
   Now all suspect,
For politics hold fast the sway.

Full of ambition and of pride,
Would Parliament itself o'er ride ;
   Railways control,
   Police enrol,
   Behold the goal
For which it moves at rapid stride !

O'er the music halls it lingers,
And would regulate the singers;
　　With greedy eye,
　　In each man's pie
　　Would like to try
And insert its greasy fingers.

Our water it would bring from Wales,
Though great expense such scheme entails;
　　But what care they?
　　I need not say
　　The public pay
Out of the rate that never fails.

On tramways, it is simply mad,
And if a statement could be had
　　Methinks 'twould show
　　How losses grow,
　　For all must know
The risk attending such a fad.

They want to build ('tis past a laugh)—
'Twill cost two millions and a-half—
　　Close to the Strand,
　　I understand;
　　But nought's too grand
To hold the Council and its staff.

Larger, and larger, thus it grows,
Where it will end, no person knows;
　　Rights invading,
　　Civic trading,
　　Ever craving
To "boss" all London's sights and shows.

UNDERGROUND RAILWAY.

———

Wife and I one day were found,
Railway station, underground ;
   Bustle and squeeze,
   Both ill at ease,
   " Stand back please,"
Then we heard that well known sound—

" Victoria train this way,
" Third forward," much push and sway :
   Here take my arm,
   Now pray be calm;
   " Hurry up, Marm,"
Bang, bang, then " right away ! "

Somehow we are left behind,
Proper carriage couldn't find,
   Thus had to wait,
   Next train is late,
   Great crowd at gate,
Had enough, no more inclined.

Upward mount, we there remain,
Glad to quit the horrid train ;
   With little fuss,
   Jump in a bus,
   Our woes discuss,
So we travel home again.

THE VILLAGE COBBLER.

The village cobbler is a useful man,
Dispense with his services if you can;
From the early morn a-beating his lap,
Was heard the hammer of Christopher Strap.
A wizen old man, some sixty and five,
To earn a fair living did most contrive;
For two or three months he'd work like a slave,
And just like an orderly " snob " behave;
Then all of a sudden would break away
From the paths of temperance, sad to say,
And in this state some days continue,
Not working a bone, muscle or sinew.
On occasion such as I've portrayed,
From his home, the restless cobbler had strayed.
It was getting dark, he did not return,
Thus causing his wife the greatest concern;
Then donning her shawl she hastened abroad,
Enquiries to make for her missing lord.
To the likeliest place she did repair,
Viz., a roadside Inn, called the " Old Brown Bear ";
He'd been in and out many times that day,
The landlord expressed his regret to say,
Mine host's politeness was much like his beer—
Pleasant to behold but thin as veneer.
Strap appeared to have left an hour ago,
With as much beer on board as he could stow.
Kind friends and neighbours to the rescue came,
And began to hunt for their human game:
Searching with lanterns each footpath and ditch,
For the night though hot, was as dark as pitch;
But 'twas labour lost, for no trace was found,
And many surmised that the man was drowned.
Now a funeral taking place next day,
The Sexton to the Churchyard made his way
To inspect and see that all was ready

To receive the corpse they had to bury.
By an open grave, while standing alone,
Beneath his feet issued forth a groan ;
Though by nature brave he received a shock,
'Twas enough to shake the firmest rock.
With courage restored he looked in the gap,
And there, just awake, found Christopher Strap.
It appears he thought he was homeward bound,
But blundered into the burial ground ;
His unsteady legs now much trouble gave,
And he fell headlong down an open grave,
And swore when he found himself within it,
At the rate of twenty d——s a minute.
Getting tired of that, in a drunken sleep
At the bottom laid, a misshapen heap.
When before the Bench he begged for pardon,
Trusting his fault they would not be hard on.
The Mayor remarked with a serious air—
That it certainly was a " grave " affair ;
But as misery had been his portion,
They dismissed him with the usual caution.

THE OMNIBUS CONDUCTOR.

Pity the man behind the bus,
A life of worry, toil and fuss ;
   He's kept awake
   With tug and shake,
   He dare not make
A protest, or show animus.

The buses every day contain—
The testy, foolish and urbane ;
   Through snub or slight,
   Must be polite,
   Or some will write
Straight to the office and complain.

Stupid people are a trial,
This fact admits of no denial,
 Hardly knowing
 Where they're going,
 Often showing
Impatience if they wait awhile.

They hail a bus that's City bound,
When they have settled down 'tis found
 They want to go
 To Earl's Court Show,
 Or Rotten Row,
Or perhaps the Oval cricket ground.

They 've never change, needs scarce be told,
For penny fares they proffer gold,
 But what is worse,
 They lose their purse,
 Should bring their nurse
To keep their cash and parcels hold

Anxious to reach their own abode,
Some people stop him on the road,
 Half-way up hill,
 Enough to kill
 The horses, till
They pant and stagger 'neath the load.

With a scale of moderate pay,
The hours are long, no time to play ;
 He mounts the stairs,
 Then down repairs,
 Collect the fares
A hundred times or so a day.

WINTRY WEATHER.

The farmer took a glance around
And thus spake he, with voice profound:
"Look smart, my lads and lassies all,
For snow will soon begin to fall.
Now, Jerry, see the cattle housed,
And, Phœbe, have your wits aroused."
This, to the pretty dairy-maid,
A glance at whom is well repaid:
Black, wayward curls in loose array
About her forehead wanton play;
Brown, laughing eyes, which seem to speak,
Illume a rosy, dimpled cheek;
White, glistening teeth, of matchless form,
Dazzle and take the eye by storm;
Her sleeves tucked up, and out of harm,
Display a plump and mottled arm.
For, busy like the rest is she
Preparing for the enemy.
The pump is bound with wisps of straw
To keep it in a state of thaw;
Much water's drawn and firewood stacked,
With food for stock in shelters packed;
Thrown o'er his house, to make him snug,
The watch-dog has a sack or rug.
The cold is getting more intense,
Frost-spangled now is every fence;
The poultry feel the bitter wind—
Obtain what shelter they can find,
And many from the yard retreat
To seek the cowshed's grateful heat.
The horsepond, shaded by the trees,
Is edged with ice, and soon will freeze;
Dull, leaden clouds dark threatening grow,
And next day all is wrapped in snow.

THE LIGHTSHIP.

It is a wild and stormy night
   Which makes the casement rattle
The wind and rain in angry fight,
Each trying to assert its right
   In long-contested battle.

Far out at sea—five miles, or more—
   While we are soundly sleeping,
Encircled by the constant roar
Of fretful billows breaking o'er,
   Stout hearts their watch are keeping.

A lightship riding through the gale,
   Its flashlight ever turning ;
The sturdy crew will never fail,
Confined as in a floating gaol,
   To keep its light a-burning.

Hark ! to the sound of signal gun—
   It is the lightship's warning ;
Quite helpless to avoid or shun,
Some vessel on the sands has run,
   There to await the morning.

On yonder hill, the eye may catch
   A small cottage it embowers,
With white-washed walls and roof of thatch,
Surrounded by a garden patch
   Ablaze with simple flowers.

Within, a wife and bairns are fed—
   Whose wants are ever growing—
The latter, fast asleep in bed,
The former, by strict duties led,
   Is busy at her sewing.

The wind, still moaning round the trees,
　Awakens not the sleepers ;
But she, poor creature, ill at ease ;
Her husband's work is on the seas—
　One of the lightship keepers.

In peering through the open air
　To watch the light revolving,
She sees at length the welcome flare
Which tells her that her loved one's there,
　All anxious doubts dissolving.

Morn ushers in a cloudless day,
　It seems a new creation ;
The wind and rain have passed away,
The sparkling waves are dancing gay
　In joyous emulation.

A lifeboat now appears in sight,
　Towards the harbour making ;
She has on board a goodly few
Belonging to a ship-wrecked crew
　Whose vessel fast is breaking.

After the storm, now o'er and past,
　The lightship's safely lying ;
'Tis painted red, with beacon mast,
While two stout anchors hold it fast—
　The elements defying.

Excitement in the cottage, see
　The children watch the weather ;
To-morrow father will be free,
And for a month off duty be
　To live with them together.

DRAPERS' SALES.

The London season is on the wane,
And folks will soon leave town again ;
Like shoals of herrings, to and fro,
From sea to sea they come and go.
The wily drapers, knowing this,
Are anxious not these fish to miss ;
They spread their nets, and cast their bait,
For which the issue they await.
A circular arrives by post
While you discuss your breakfast toast;
Outside it says : " Great clearance sale,"
With minor facts of much detail.
In it you read, with some dismay,
That goods are being thrown away,
Regardless of the cost and price,
At most alarming sacrifice ;
You're asked to come without delay
On what they call the " remnant day."
In female circles, much comment
Is made upon this document,
And, forming couples, they agree
Not to buy, but just to call and see.
Having partaken of a chop,
They hasten to the draper's shop ;
There, struggling to get in, they find
A heated mass of womankind.
'Tis a strange and curious sight
To see the ladies almost fight
O'er the pile of goods strewn around—
The cheapest bargains ever found.
Now, what to purchase doth perplex
These members of the gentler sex ;
Blouses, skirtings, frills and laces,
Scrutinised by anxious faces.

Their minds made up, they now retire
With lots of things they don't require,
Returning home with empty purse,
And parcels in their arms to nurse ;
But most of them contrive to be
Back in time for their husband's tea ;
With pride then forth their bargains spread,
Their spouse says naught, but shakes his head.

DUSTMEN.

Of those who cleanse and tidy keep
  The thoroughfares of our city,
The dustman, scavenger and sweep
  Are the three I greatly pity.

The dustmen, I'm inclined to think,
  Have the hardest lot of any ;
Yet from no work will mortals shrink
  To obtain an honest penny.

Mid'st dirt and grit of putrid soil,
  And all sorts of impurity,
Do these hard workers slave and toil ;
  Their effort's our security.

Bacteria exist, they say,
  Where we least expect to find them,
Which these poor men inhale each day,
  And yet never seem to mind them.

If germ theories be correct,
  On which many place reliance,
Why do they not dustmen affect ?
  I would ask the man of science.

ELOQUENCE.

How oft the world is borne away
  More by eloquence than reason ?
Many a wretch has had to pay
  For listening to rash treason.

The man who has the gift of speech,
  On publicly appearing,
What'er the doctrine he may teach
  Will rarely lack a hearing.

The agitator of the day
  Will ever have a following;
Poor working men are led astray,
  And undergo much sorrowing.

Men, loving repartee and jest,
  Will respond with cheers most hearty;
And he who's found to talk the best
  Is made leader of their party.

We, in our time, have seen, alas !
  A strange and wondrous spectacle:
A *statesman of the highest class,
  Whose speeches were electrical.

For changing tactics, so inclined,
  That no principles could bind him;
He mystified the public mind,
  And confusion left behind him.

In search of truth I seldom roam,
  Though some may call me heretic;
'Tis surely best to read at home
  Than be enslaved by rhetoric ?

        * Mr. W. E. Gladstone.

CHARITY.

The greatest of the virtues three,
We all are told is Charity.
A plant that often blossoms late,
Yet we do well to cultivate.
Press writers now their talents waste
In pandering to the public taste ;
On small pretext some tale relate
A public scandal to create.
On demand, supply will follow ;
In this case to our great sorrow.
Remember this, no one is free
From censure or from calumny :
And people you will ever find,
Whose tongue no human power can bind ;
Before your face they courage lack,
Though talk of you behind your back—
Perhaps at the very time when you
Regard them as your friends most true.
To slander lend no ready ear—
Believe not half that you may hear.
One tale's good till another's told—
A saying quite as true as old.
From this we may a lesson learn,
Before we judge, hear each in turn.
As the chariot wheels of time
Roll on through every land and clime,
Its foaming horses do not stop,
E'en to let the traveller drop,
Who, standing on that distant shore,
Is deaf to censure ever more.
The bustling world disturbs him not,
And soon his presence is forgot,
Except amongst a chosen few
Of loving hearts, devout and true—
In whose memory long may he
Be blessed by thee, sweet Charity.

NATIONAL CHARACTERISTICS.

A Scot and Briton took a walk
With an Irish friend, new from Cork;
Passing a shop, the trio spied
A pretty girl who served inside.
" Let us spend half-a-crown," said Pat,
" And with her have a pleasant chat."
The Briton said, " Don't be a muff ;
A shilling will be quite enough."
The thrifty Scot exclaimed, " Nae, nae!
We'll all go in and ask the way
To Charing Cross, or where you will,
And then we'll get our talk for nil."

THE JOURNEY OF LIFE.

Man's years are the mile-stones on the highway of life,
Which seem to stand closer t'wards the end of his strife;
For oft on the journey there are trials enough,
The footpath's uneven, the roads stony and rough ;
But a great deal depends on ourselves, it is true,
To make the way pleasant by the course we pursue.
'Tis labour and sorrow to the stricken in health,
Who would gladly exchange or surrender their wealth
To obtain a relief from the tortures of pain,
For while worn by disease they seek pleasure in vain ;
Some travellers succumb before reaching their prime—
Are often forgotten in the whirlwind of time.
The keen frost of winter the weak infant will seize,
And cast down the aged like leaves from the trees ;
Some, favoured by fortune, will move joyous along,
Escaping the troubles which to others belong,
But few in their number, when compared with the rest,
Whose lot is a struggle, an existence at best ;
The fastest to travel may reach quickest the gaol,
But life fail to enjoy as the slow, plodding soul.

GUDGEON FISHING.

'Tis August; weather sultry, hot;
Town forsaken, almost forgot.
Three angling friends had long agreed
To have a day at Runnymead,
Where, for ten thousand years or so,
The Thames had never ceased to flow,
Whose silvery waters joy impart
To lovers of the gentle art.
They fix the day, the punt engage,
Their fisherman doth strong presage
That should the wind continue west
They of good sport will have the best;
Each, sitting in his Windsor chair,
Puts to his rod and line with care.
Then, softly gliding down the stream,
They stop where fish are known to teem;
Push in the poles, the punt make fast,
Plumb the depth, the lines in cast.
Now, gudgeon fishing oft provokes
Much merriment, good-natured jokes;
The custom is to have three bets—
A shilling each to him who gets
The first that's taken in the fray,
The largest caught throughout the day;
The third reward to him will go
Who can the greatest number show.
" I've got first fish! 'tis very plain;
By jove! it's fallen in again."
A shout of laughter greeting this;
It was a most provoking miss.
At length a victim's brought to bank,
His health, of course, is duly drank;
The fish are madly " on the feed,"
Our friends are busy now, indeed.

But **they in turn** require a bite
To stay **their** craving appetite ;
The luncheon basket soon unpacked,
The cloth is spread and nothing lacked :
Lobster salad with pigeon pie,
And bottled Bass to cheer the eye ;
After that, by way of pastry,
Genoa cake, rich and tasty.
Then all light up the fragrant weed,
And to their floats give little heed ;
Far away in the land of Nod,
Now worship they the drowsy god,
Till someone starts up in a fright,
Wondering if it's day or night ;
For where he is, he scarce can tell
Till objects round his dreams dispel.
The trio now are wide awake,
Their man begins to use the rake,
For should the gravel be well stirred
It makes the stream look thick and blurred ;
Then prowling gudgeons, swimming near,
Towards the clouded water steer,
Eager their favourite food to find,
So to the fatal hook are blind.
The bobbing floats now clearly tell
That fish again are biting well ;
The shadows from the poplar trees
Now disappear as sunlight flees,
The martins swarm the withey bed,
While homeward rooks pass overhead.
Each angler now withdraws his line,
To clear away they all combine ;
The fish are reckoned up and weighed,
Bets are owned and promptly paid.
Thus ends a happy, pleasant day,
In their memories long to stay.

SPRING.

All Nature beams with grateful praise,
   The springtide's sun is shining
At winter's dark and gloomy days,
   Men's hearts will cease repining.

The joyous larks are heard on high,
   Towards heaven's portals rising,
Sweet minstrels of our northern sky,
   The songs of earth despising.

The feathered tribe, with rapture filled,
   By instinct strongly guided;
Their mates to choose, their nest to build,
   Are cares to them confided.

The partridge, jealous of his spouse,
   Will from all eyes exclude her,
And then to mortal combat rouse
   A thoughtless, gay intruder.

The hedgerows now are tinged with green,
   The blackthorn bloom is fading,
The early bracken's also seen
   The forest-land invading.

Once more appears in swamps and dells
   Marsh-mallow's golden cluster,
Whose gorgeous brightness far excels
   All other flowers in lustre.

The hum of bees falls on the ear
   In gardens long forsaken,
While swarms of insect life appear
   From winter's trance to waken.

Messrs. WHITE & PRICE

(On receiving from them a box of Spanish Onions).

My thanks for the onions, White & Price,
Though not so fragrant as Eastern spice,
They oft my appetite will tickle,
Specially if prepared as pickle,
Which will make me better, say my grace,
Eat cold mutton with a smiling face,
Instead of calling it naughty names,
Or darkly frown on the stale remains;
With customers' tempers thus improved,
May orders follow thy pungent food.

WHITE & PRICE.

Garlic, shallots, onions Spanish
Quickly cause cold meat to vanish,
Impart a flavour and a zest
When appetites are not the best;
Should I indulge in Irish stew,
A fricandeau or rich ragout,
So useful will your present be
Which you have kindly sent to me;
The warmest thanks I can bestow
Will fail my gratitude to show.

IDLENESS.

Amongst the busy men we see
  Who pour into the City,
An idle warehouse clerk shall be
  The subject of my ditty.

He was a pleasant sort of youth—
  Small moustache, with curly hair ;
He had, to tell the honest truth,
  But little of brains to spare.

No energy to make amends
  For his intellect so slow ;
Hard work and he had parted friends,
  A very long time ago.

When all were busy taking stock,
  He never moved the faster ;
But kept one eye on the clock,
  The other on the master.

Of work he'd sometimes make a show,
  But the effort died away :
To wash his hands, he'd slip below
  Some five or six times a day.

With cane in hand, and glass at eye,
  A scarf of gorgeous silk,
Once, coming late, he made reply
  " I was waiting for the milk!"

A hindrance to his fellow clerk,
  His dismissal was no loss ;
It came when he had left his work
  To indulge in pitch and toss.

HOUSE PAINTING.

The dog, the cat and I agree,
And everybody else will see,
To paint your house in early spring
What great discomfort it doth bring.
The weather's cold for Eastertide,
Yet every window's open wide;
I, from the upper rooms, retire
To sit beside the kitchen fire.
The cat has gone to see a friend—
May not return till matters mend;
The dog sticks to his master's heels,
And plainly tells him what he feels
By fitful barks and smothered growl
When e'er he hears the noisy trowel;
Evidently he takes it ill
To hear the frequent shouts of "Bill!"
Why this name should so common be
'Mongst working men has puzzled me.
Now is the time for "Mr. Sikes"
To gain an entrance if he likes;
Ladders and steps, with coils of rope,
The burglar's mind would fill with hope.
I often think, when I'm in bed,
I hear strange footsteps overhead;
The thing is pressing on my mind,
And yet I ought no fault to find,
The work's progressing, so to speak,
And will be finished in a week.
The end has come, the men clear out,
I'm "through the wood," and now may shout;
My pleasure I can scarce retain,
For "Richard is himself again."
Puss, in a scratched and shabby state,
Sits in front of the kitchen grate;
The dog is sleeping at my feet,
And all are glad the job's complete.

BANJO BAY.

Many weeks of anxious toil,
Burning much the midnight oil,
Thought I'd like to change the soil,
 So to seaside went;
Banjo Bay, my home I made,
Number 6, the Grand Parade,
Three guineas a week I paid
 As a ground floor rent.

If I wanted peace and rest,
Rooms of which I'd been in quest,
Certainly these were the best,
 I was strictly told;
Took possession, had my tea—
Shrimps, of course, fresh from the sea—
Felt as happy as could be,
 When my blood ran cold:

An open fly is at the door,
A man, his wife and children four,
Come to take the upper floor—
 What am I to do?
Up and down the stairs they run,
Full of frolic, life and fun,
I quite feel that I've been done,
 Betwixt me and you.

There's a bouncing overhead,
Cries when they are put to bed—
This is what I got instead
 Of peace and quiet!
Baby's fallen from the cot,
Some one has a spanking got,
Woe is my unhappy lot
 To have this riot.

One unpleasant thing I found,
Youngsters bring the niggers round,
And the horrid, buzzing sound
    Of hurdy-gurdy ;
Barrel organs, in the street,
Now the same old tunes repeat,
Whilst minstrel bands make complete
    The hurly-burly.

Longer here I will not stay,
Fear my brain is giving way,
What I have endured this day
    Preys upon my mind ;
Far inland I mean to go,
Where the hops and barley grow,
And they reckon life is slow—
    Best suits me, I find.

If you're feeling well and strong,
Want a change, you can't do wrong,
Join the laughing, giddy throng
    Where the niggers play ;
If much worry's been your share,
Feel you want a blow of air,
To some peaceful place repair
    Far from Banjo Bay.

OUTWARD BOUND.

A powerful ship lies deep in the Docks,
The finest of craft e'er launched from the stocks,
Capacious and large, yet graceful in shape ;
To-morrow at noon she'll steam for the Cape ;
Her passenger list is full and complete,—
Twelve hundred of souls together will meet.
Strange the assortment, in varied attire,
Pray who may they be ? let's seek to enquire :
Doctors and nurses *en route* for the war,
Two or three bankrupts evading the law ;
Officers chatting in grand saloon,
Are whiling away a dull afternoon ;
Sandhurst or Woolwich has furnished no doubt
These light-hearted lads now being sent out.
A party of men for smartness well-known,
Discussing some point in an undertone,
Are mining experts and bound for the " rand "
New ventures to start, old ones to expand.
Investors too oft are blind in their greed,
And follow such men wherever they lead,
Finding, like pigeons, that hawks swift and strong
Pluck off their feathers before very long.
That " ne'er to do well " and troublesome son,
A plague to his friends and comfort to none,
Is sent once again to that remote shore,
May be to return a trial once more.
The thoughtful young girl clad neatly in grey,
A lover to join is now on her way,
He, travelling far o'er the ocean wide,

Has founded a home for his faithful bride.
The consumptive youth, now pacing the deck,
With thick woollen scarf encircling his neck,
Is ordered abroad, let's hope in good time,
To cure his disease in sunnier clime.
This family group next let us observe :
A Cornish-bred man with an iron nerve,
Sturdy are all his three children and wife—
Fit subjects indeed for emigrant life.
Domestic servants, some thirty or more,
Conducted by those who watch o'er the poor,
Will, when they arrive, good wages obtain,
Or marry, perchance, some prosperous swain.
A hundred or so of soldiers on board,
To fill up the ranks of regiments abroad.
Carpenters, masons, and miners a score,
Off to prospect the land of the Boer.
The time has arrived for making a start—
The mails are on deck and friends all depart;
Leaving the basin to enter the stream,
She's hauled by the tugs all fluster and steam,
With the ropes cast off by an active crew,
Begins to revolve her ponderous screw.
Midst shouts of good-bye, the cheering grows mad,
A gaiety forced, by hearts that are sad.
Good ship carry safe thy cargo of care,
May joy succeed hope and banish despair.

HAY-MAKING.

—.

Delightful is the time of year
When golden buttercups appear
And make the fields look joyous, blythe,
Until the mower plies his scythe :
Commencing at an early hour,
Before the sun asserts its power,
He swings his body to and fro
And brings the mass of herbage low,
Soft perfumes then the senses greet
From cowslip, clover, meadow-sweet,
Which cut down by the ruthless blade,
Yield up their fragrance e'er they fade.
Much anxious care pervades the farm
Until the hay be safe from harm ;
The master bustles up his folk,
And to his daughter Bess he spoke :
The grass is being cut to-day,
And quickly must be turned to hay,
Get all the hands that you can find—
Neighbours or friends of every kind,
To help to gather in the crop
Before the rain should chance to drop.
A fine and handsome girl is Bess,
Her to portray, let me digress :
A trifle tall, robust and strong,
Yet graceful as she moves along ;
Thick coils of hair of flaxen hue,
In quantity possessed by few ;
Forehead of high and broad expanse,
Her countenance doth much enhance ;
Expressive eyes set wide apart,

Which show, 'tis said, an open heart;
Complexion like the softest cream,
Her teeth, a marvel, and a dream.
Soon quite a little band is found
Of volunteers from all around,
Each armed with wooden fork or rake,
Proceed at once the hay to make;
Then lifting up the swath with care,
Toss, and expose it to the air.
They work until the solar heat
Compels them all to beat retreat
And seek a cool and sheltered place
To rest awhile and talk apace;
A wind now rustles through the trees,
And pleasant is the welcome breeze,
Their work the toilers then renew
Till Phœbus bids the earth adieu.
Well favoured by the wind and sun,
The harvest now is fairly won,
Placed at a corner of the field,
A massive stack contains its yield.

BOURNEMOUTH.

Amongst the south coast towns I've seen,
Bournemouth is aptly call a queen,
And merits this encomium.
   Far along the beach
   As the eye can reach
Presents a gay symposium.

There, amateurs with faces masked
Give entertainments quite unasked,
And oft deserves opprobrium.
   Crowding now begins
   Round a man who sings
And thumps an old harmonium.

The rattle of the nigger's bones,
Their cheery song of varied tones,
Meet with a just eulogium.
   While Punch and Judy,
   Sankey and Moody,
Complete the pandemonium.

Hundreds of little naked feet
Run to and fro the waves to meet,
Form nature's true emporium.
   Rest without alloy,
   Elder folks enjoy
Within this sanatorium.

LOVE'S LAMENTATIONS
(Extracted from MSS. written many years ago).

———

Dark and dreary,
Tired and weary,
Behold my soul to-day,
With bated breath,
A living death,
Can this be love I pray?

I restless fret,
And can't forget,
The day but late gone by—
When Dorothy
First smiled on me,
A sunbeam from the sky.

Its for the best,
You may suggest,
Though pain I must endure,
My wound I feel
Will never heal,
'Tis past all earthly cure.

Hard to be born,
I could have sworn
Naught but our souls could sever;
My heart is wrung,
Its chords unstrung,
Love, good-bye for ever.

———

Love, thou art the disturber
And worry of our lives;
Love, thou art an usurper,
'Gainst which one vainly strives.

Why did'st thou my soul enslave
  When Corisande appeared,
Why was not my heart more brave,
  No! coward like I feared.

Now a prisoner am I,
  Held by a silken chain ;
To escape I dare not try,
  And powerless to complain.

So thus I am borne along,
  Midst sunshine, cloud and rain ;
Love the ruling passion strong,
  Which bringeth naught but pain.

SERVIA, 1903.

—

The people place a youth in power,
  Of wisdom, not the essence ;
Assassins chose the midnight hour
  To rid them of his presence.

Hands stained with blood of Queen and King,
  Rejoice they in the murder,
And flock to Church, Te Deums sing—
  Can blasphemy go further ?

I'd rather be of honest toil,
  Peasant in Hibernia,
Or one who ploughs the British soil
  Than a king in Servia.

THE HUNT.

We hold to-day our opening " Meet "
At Barton Court, the Master's seat;
    With weather bright,
    A pleasing sight,
    Gives much delight,
New friends to make, old ones to greet.

The breakfast o'er, the guests prepare
To join the crowd assembled there ;
    Ladies are found
    Gathering round
    Huntsmen and hound,
Much fun prevailing everywhere.

The time arrives to make a start,
As hounds pass through we stand apart,
    Then jog along,
    A laughing throng—
    Some fifty strong,
Off to the nearest woods depart.

'Midst dead leaves and tangled bracken,
Hounds their efforts do not slacken :
    With heads deflect,
    And tails erect,
    We all expect
Early news our hearts to gladden.

A dog gives tongue, relieves our doubts,
We hear the horn and welcome shouts
    Of " View, Hulloa,"
    Away we go,
    Excitement show,
Trying to find the whereabouts.

Soon each one settles in his place,
Leaving the fox to make the pace,
    Pack well in front
    Now leave the hunt
    To. bear the brunt
Of hedge and ditch, a steeplechase.

Some say the Doctor's had a spill,
While others think 'tis lawyer Gill ;
    Which of the pair
    We best can spare
    I won't declare,
Let those decide who have the will.

Now the pace becomes severe,
Many are left far in the rear,
    Some dogs grow slack,
    And dropping back
    From wearied pack,
In a long straggling line appear.

Towards Croftside Spinney onward rush,
There all our hopes receive a crush :
    We search each drain,
    But quite in vain,
    'Tis very plain
That master Fox has saved his brush.

THE SIEGE.

It is a gruesome time of war,
  When great hostile armies meet,
And peaceful men are kept in awe,
For everywhere there's martial law
  To make misery complete.

Sinister news imparts a shock,
  Which ominous signs confirm ;
The farmers' men drive in their stock,
Towards the town the peasants flock
  With their aged and infirm.

These wretched folk quit their abode
  Struck with terror and dismay ;
Their laden carts choke up the road,
The enemy, as some forbode,
  Being scarce ten miles away.

See yonder hills, once bright arrayed
  With the mustard's yellow bloom,
While fields of purple clover made
A brilliant scene of light and shade
  With patches of golden broom.

A mighty host to camp is come
  And has devastated all ;
The tinkling bell of sheep is dumb,
And naught is heard but roll of drum
  Or the ring of bugle call.

Beneath the tread of horse and men
  Is the tender floweret crushed ;
Rabbits with fright have fled the glen,
The startled fox has left his den,
  And the song bird's notes are hushed.

The gallant town is under arms
   And entrenched on every side ;
The constant scare of night alarms,
And lurid glare of burning farms,
   Sad excitement doth provide.

Now, outposts, keep ye watch and guard
   To give warning of attack,
And if the foe should press ye hard,
Ye'll try his progress to retard
   And gradually fall back.

The roar of gun, the burst of shell,
   With the crash of falling roof ;
The constant shower of shot that fell,
The mournful toll of the fire bell
   Put men's courage to the proof.

The siege drags on, much blood is shed,
   And the end seems drawing nigh ;
For smaller gets our dole of bread,
Though lack of water most we dread,
   For the wells are almost dry.

Although closed in, this comfort feel,
   We're not by the world forgot ;
The topic of its morning meal,
At night the silent prayers appeal
   For our sad and lonely lot.

One early morn, no foe we see,
   While sounds like distant thunder
Prove British guns have set us free,
And make our town to England be
   Its glory and its wonder.

AMERICAN SMALL REPUBLICS.

—

[The whole of these small Republics have from time to time borrowed
money on our Stock Exchange; the majority of them are in
default—that is to say, unable to pay the interest on their
bonds, which, in several instances, are regarded as worthless.]

—

These petty states, no need to name,
    By honest men resented;
Their goings on are much the same—
    A sample's here presented:

Blood of Indians, Spaniards, Dutch—
    Strange mixture to inherit;
The State on which I now would touch
    Has neither cash nor credit.

To raise a loan, all means it tried
    On pretext soft as honey;
Then to our Stock Exchange applied,
    And so obtained the money.

This money did more harm than good,
    In civil war expended;
Its chiefs shed all the blood they could
    In quarrels never ended.

Then came a falling off in trade,
    Pledged was public property;
While much of honour made parade,
    Pompous in its poverty.

We to a smaller power defer,
    Yielding to their impotence;
'Twas lost upon this snarling cur,
    Who the more showed insolence.

Inflated, swelled like Æsop's frog,
  Its boasting naught could fetter ;
Like "Brag," 'twas thought a splendid dog
  Till "Holdfast" proved the better.

For with our patience overwrought,
  No more indulgence granting,
We send the fleet to seize a port
  And guarantees demanding.

THE FOX.

The fox enjoys a bad repute,
For reasons one can scarce refute ;
A burglar, footpad, thief is he,
Sly and cunning as he can be.
By nature not a family man,
His wife contrives as best she can
To live alone and educate
The youngsters of her faithless mate,
Who, on a clear and moonlight night,
Are seen engaged in mimic fight ;
Amusing little chaps are they,
Like kittens in their sportive play.
'Tis time they now commenced to learn
Their business and their food to earn ;
So, when the night is well advanced,
And all the world's in sleep entranced,
They follow at their mother's heels,
Who through the coverts softly steals.
Of choice of supper none have they,
" Pot luck's " the order of the day ;
Perhaps a rabbit, young and fat,

A hedgehog or a woodland rat ;
But should the woods afford no sport,
Not e'en a pheasant to be caught,
They'll to some farmhouse wend their way
In search of more forbidden prey,
And oftentimes will have the luck
To pounce upon a sleeping duck ;
Or, failing that, with hunger keen,
May in the poultry yard be seen.
Should unsecured the fowlhouse be,
Then will ensue a tragedy ;
Whether he wants the fowls or not
A fox will soon destroy the lot ;
Next morn the birds will oft be found
Half buried in the fields around.
When falling leaves the trees deface,
Ere Winter shows her withered face,
The huntsman scours the woods and scrubs
To blood the hounds, disperse the cubs ;
Thus each young fox is sent adrift,
In future for himself to shift.

HOMEWARD BOUND.

Home has a magic sound to those
  Who abroad their time have squandered,
And long once more to seek repose
  In the land from whence they've wandered.

A noble ship lies in the bay,
  Her departure signal flying,
And now she slowly steams away,
  On her power and strength relying.

She carries quite a little town
  Of people in variety,
Who very quickly settle down,
  And choose their own society.

There is a famous man on board,
  Who's reached the greatest altitude
Of rank that England can accord
  To soldiers in her gratitude.

Has fought our battles since a boy,
  And made a name in history ;
He comes in triumph to enjoy
  The well earned fruits of victory.

Up-country farmers—sturdy, strong—
  A few traders, rich and thriving,
On deck, in groups together throng,
  Old acquaintanceships reviving.

Yon stands a man, good health denied,
  Has left his wife and family ;
A long sea voyage now has tried
  To cure him of his malady.

War invalids our numbers swell,
  Who in hard campaigns have laboured ;
Although all did their duty well
  They were not by fortune favoured.

Broken in health, return on leave,
  Their condition each one pities :
No sword of honour to receive
  Nor the freedom of ten cities.

But gifts, more precious far than these,
  Are awaiting their arrival,
Fond loving hearts their hands to seize
  In affection's strong revival.

The passengers are all astir
  And great activity prevails ;
Their packing many will defer,
  Hurried labour this entails.

Men run on deck and swarm the sides
  Like children from a boarding-school,
As, favoured by the wind and tides,
  The ship draws near to Liverpool.

A vessel 'gainst the jetty leans,
  Where her postal bags are landed ;
Comes rush of friends, affecting scenes,
  And our company is disbanded.

FOUL CHIMNEYS.

I'm sitting in my easy chair
  And giving way to lazing,
When all at once there comes a scare,
I to the kitchen straight repair
  To find the chimney blazing.

Confusion reigns, I need not say,
  Our cook is much excited;
The ladies, half afraid to stay,
Pack up their things to fly away
  In case the house ignited.

I ascertain how matters stand
  On due examination:
Send for the sweep, who's close at hand,
He soon arrives with sacks and sand
  To put out the conflagration.

My hands are full, I here may state,
  The housemaid's in convulsions,
A crowd of boys makes me irate,
I haste to lock the garden gate
  After a few expulsions.

A shout is raised of " Here it comes ! "
  Engine from the fire brigade,
Followed by loafers and their chums,
While swarms of children from the slums
  Our good neighbourhood invade.

A fire escape arrives at last
  Amidst some cheers and laughter,
Though the machine can travel fast,
It oft appears when danger's past
  And then retires soon after.

By firemen, turncock, policemen, sweep,
  The fire's at length got under ;
The crowd, with disappointment deep,
Slowly disperse, though children keep
  Still gazing up in wonder.

By tips and drinks, I made all straight,
  As I artfully supposed,
And yet I had not long to wait
Before a summons sealed my fate—
  Twenty shillings fine imposed.

Asked when the chimney last was swept,
  One thought 'twas in November ;
But nothing could I hear, except
'Twas clear no record had been kept
  And no one could remember.

This matter caused us much distress—
  You'll understand my meaning ;
To see the house in such a mess
Was very vexing, you may guess,
  Just after our spring cleaning.

THE POLICEMAN.

" Man in his time plays many parts,"
　　So wrote our greatest poet;
This saying much of truth imparts,
Touches our official hearts,
　　And I'll proceed to show it:

I'm Policeman Jones (19 B),
　　And when you hear my statement
You will, I think, with me agree,
It's truth of what I do and see
　　Admits of no abatement.

The smartest man you ever saw,
　　E'en in the rank of " sogers,"
I give advice, explain the law,
And listen to the endless jaw
　　Of loud, disputing lodgers.

To ladies I'm polite, you're sure,
　　And help them o'er the crossing;
I find lost " kids," stray dogs allure,
Try bolting horses to secure
　　When traffic rules enforcing.

When winter's nights are cold and damp,
　　Awake at early morning,
You'll hear my footsteps solemn tramp,
See the flash of my bull's-eye lamp
　　To give all burglars warning.

If thus upon my beat at night
　　I find a window open,
The folks I wake up in a fright,
Tell them their fastenings are not right—
　　Result: a liquid token !

To regulate the traffic, means
  A constant life of bully ;
You have to give the driver " beans,"
This sometimes leads to angry scenes
  Which tries your temper fully.

" Point " duty is, I need not say,
  Devoid of all enjoyment ;
You're fixed to one dull spot all day,
From which you dare not move away,
  Or forfeit your employment.

When placed upon a West-End beat
  You pick up many stray pence ;
But in the East you lose that treat,
With roughest treatment often meet
  And get more kicks than ha'pence.

" Now, gentlemen, pass along, please "—
  Our West-End exhortation ;
But at an East-end crowd or squeeze
It's " Move on, there!" then one you seize
  And run him in the station.

But that which I like best of all
  Is cheerful occupation ;
To keep the footway at a ball,
And help the carriages to call,
  Means good remuneration.

The grass ne'er grows beneath my feet,
  So I'm exceeding busy,
Securing tips from the *élite*,
Then getting something nice to eat,
  With oft a drop of " fizzy."

Now, in a kitchen down below
  There lives a little beauty ;
The cook's divine, full well I know,
To chat with her I often go—
  " Of course," when not on duty.

Her mistress once brought me to book ;
  Then, with a tale most thrilling :
" 'Gainst thieves I'd come to warn her cook ;"
" Quite right," said she, with smiling look,
  And handed me a shilling.

Well versed in every kind of crime,
  And thought a good detector,
And though I have not reached my prime,
I hope to be, in course of time,
  A good police inspector.

CHRISTMAS CARD, 1902.

—

I post to you and each dear friend
   My Christmas salutation,
And with it all good wishes send,
That health and happiness attend
   A life of long duration.

When clouds beneath a stormy sky
   Around your household gather,
May you be strengthened from on high
The powers of evil to defy
   And cause those clouds to scatter.

With peace restored, the coming year
   Should be a joyous morrow ;
Oh ! may it have a bright career,
And cost you not a single tear,
   Nor rend your heart with sorrow.

———

Lightning Source UK Ltd.
Milton Keynes UK
UKHW010632091218
333661UK00004B/220/P